I0548791

THE END TIDE

CARRION VIRUS #3

M.W. DUNCAN

SEVERED PRESS
HOBART TASMANIA

THE END TIDE

Copyright © 2017 M.W. Duncan

WWW.SEVEREDPRESS.COM

ISBN: 978-1-925711-34-9

ACKNOWLEDGEMENTS

This book is dedicated to Jane Appleby - you know why.

As usual there is a list of people I need to thank who have in one way or another helped with getting this book completed. It's been a long road but we did it. Huge thanks go to Pauline, Bex, Hannah, Angus, Debbie, Jon (another one for story boy), Honey and Alice. Always thanks to my friends and family for keeping me going and to everyone who has read my books. This is just the beginning. I'll see you all next time.

M. W. Duncan
September 2017

LO! Death has reared himself a throne
In a strange city lying alone
Far down within the dim West,
Where the good and the bad and the worst and the best
Have gone to their eternal rest.
There shrines and palaces and towers
(Time-eaten towers that tremble not!)
Resemble nothing that is ours.
Around, by lifting winds forgot,
Resignedly beneath the sky
The melancholy waters lie.

Edgar Allan Poe

CHAPTER 1

GREY SKIES AND ELECTRIC LIGHTS

Ryan Bannister sat on a park bench and blew into his hands to vanish the frigid cold from his fingers. It had little effect. Seattle was blanketed in snow once again, but the sun was trying to burst through the grey skies. The park was so quiet. Two walkers unclipped leashes to allow their dogs a few metres of freedom. Five determined joggers dashed past, same pace, in a line, all with headphones blocking out the din of the world. An attractive woman snapped away at winter flowers with a digital camera. She looked up from her hobby, meeting Ryan's stare, and offered a smile. He returned a nod.

But the park had not always been like that.

For the briefest moment Ryan could pretend that the world was not insane. The Carrion Virus felt a million miles away. It was only collateral changes within his city that hinted at the presence of a world catastrophe far away. Flights into the country were restricted and health checks mandatory. International travel was granted to a rare few. Police patrols had doubled. Media outlets reported a frantic strain on hospitals in the city. And very few ventured outdoors. The virus had yet to reach the US but the preceding panic was on its way.

Ryan knocked his foot against the rucksack by his feet. Plain, black and cumbersome, he eyed it with some misgiving. It held canisters to release a Carrion Virus in its airborne form. Ryan designed the canisters, and he had his orders. The Owls of Athena demanded he place the canisters strategically within the city to ensure maximum damage. He was one of thousands in the US, and one of many more around the world charged with the same task. The Athena Protocol was in place. But something had happened and now The Owls of Athena demanded the unleashing be sped up.

A Labrador sniffed at the rucksack.

1

"Get lost!" Ryan shooed the animal away with the tip of his polished shoe, then dragged the rucksack to sit between his feet.

The dog's owner offered a curt apology as she called the dog away.

The shrill whistle of Ryan's mobile rang out.

"Hello," he said.

Static burst as the call encrypted.

"That was careless leaving the bag unprotected," said the familiar voice, one that had offered orders via phone from the moment he left Japan.

"You're watching me now?" Ryan's eyes darted up and down the snow-covered streets. The dog was gone. No joggers. Everything looked monochromatic and still.

"The Owls are always watching you, lad. That bag is worth more than your life. Don't be so careless."

"Do you have a name?"

"My name is none of your concern," came the casual reply. "But perhaps you can call me Law."

"Law?"

"It is very appropriate."

"You know I spent time in The Owls' Nest? Do you know who I am?"

"Where do you think I take my orders from? You keep doing what you're told and we won't have a problem. Understand me?"

Ryan didn't reply. Why did he always find himself in predicaments? His father may have been instrumental in the creation of the virus, but he was a distant memory. He had no familial duty. It was that damn Hector Crispin who had confused him, lured him in with extravagant compliments and promises of great wealth. The one promise Ryan hoped was kept was that he be extracted to a safe location when he completed his task.

"Understand?" Law repeated.

"Yeah, I get it."

"You see the bench behind you?"

Ryan turned. Behind him, another bench, a thin layer of snow turning it into a mottled platform. An open bottle of soda sat abandoned on its arm. "What about it?"

"The bottle."

"The bottle?"

The bottle burst backwards, spinning in the air, spewing out the drink before landing in the snow behind the bench.

"I could have popped your head like a melon. We have an understanding now, don't we?"

"Yes," said Ryan, eyes on the broken bottle.

"It's time to make your first drop. I'll be in touch."

The line clicked off. Ryan locked the screen of his phone and returned it to his pocket. Part of a broken bottle's label remained intact. It was a lemon drink. The bullet had cut the neck away cleanly. Never in his life had Seattle, his home city, felt so bitter to him.

***

"We need to get down there. We need to do something," said Roy Smart.

Ash Gibbons didn't respond. He lay prone atop a sand dune, and was soaked through and shivering. The morning winds were chill in the south east of England. He stuffed a piece of gum into his mouth.

"Did you hear me? We need to get down there."

"And do what?" snapped Ash. "Fight them off with our bare hands? We'd walk into a shit storm."

"Our guys are down there!"

They had been lowered from a Russian freighter, and a small boat took the men and the cash and the firearms to shore. Their leader Brutus ordered them up the beach and onto the dunes, and they were to head further inland to meet with a contact. But an opposing force lay in wait. Brutus and the others were taken. Ash and Roy slipped through the net.

"Which is why we need to be smart," said Ash. "Look, they're dragging someone up the beach. They're here to capture us. They ain't a kill team."

"What do we do then?"

The rolling sea crashed into the beach and roared as it tried to pull land back with it.

"We've been double-crossed."

"Russians?"

"Could be. But someone knew we were coming."

"I never liked that captain. He drank too much."

"We have to find our contact," said Ash. "We can't save our men without weapons and more bodies."

"But we'll lose sight of the money."

"If you've a better suggestion, I'm all ears."

"Brutus should have handed out the weapons before we beached."

That was something Ash had thought about when the first bullet was discharged. "Yeah," he said quietly.

A noise came to their right, boots in wet sand.

Ash rolled away and Roy did likewise putting metres between them. Ash slipped over the crest of the dune on his stomach, snaking himself out of view, and hiding behind the cusp of the sandy hill. He crawled with his elbows, pulled himself along the edge of the summit. He met with a fringe of reeds and stilled.

"You found me," said Roy loudly. "I'm unarmed. Hey, there's two of you, so no need to point those things at me."

"Where is the other one?" An accent, possibly Eastern European.

"Look, I'm raising my hands. No weapons."

"Where is the other one?" came the demand again.

"What other one?" said Roy.

A dull thud was followed by Roy's famous cursing.

"Get up," ordered the voice.

Ash's hands searched for a weapon, anything, and found a rock the size of an orange. He lifted himself higher on his elbows. Two soldiers aimed MP5 submachine guns at Roy. Their backs were to Ash.

Roy pushed himself to his knees, and in that action spotted Ash. Roy looked at Ash not more than a fraction of a second then looked to the soldiers and frowned. He remained on all fours but lifted a hand to his head.

"You hit the spot with that. I'm sure there's an ostrich egg on my head." Roy rubbed the spot and cringed.

"I said get up!"

"Alright, alright." Roy moved slow and mechanically. "Give me a second will you, fellows? My head's buzzing."

Ash was upright.

Roy opened his arms. "As you can see, I'm no threat."

Ash took two slow steps forward and readied to leap.

"But if my good buddy was here, it would be—"

Ash was on top of one of the soldiers, and Roy dived forward wrapping his arms around the ankles of the other and forced him to the ground.

Ash swiped downward along the soldier's face. The soldier howled and tried to raise his MP5. From behind Ash pulled the firearm into the soldier's throat and pulled tighter and tighter. The soldier let go, leant back, reached backwards and his fingers scrambled for Ash's eyes. Ash threw his lead left and right, and pulled harder on the gun. The soldier suddenly gave up and fell to the ground. Ash raised the gun like a cricket bat and swung once. Ash panted heavily. He looked to Roy.

Roy was smiling. The handle of a combat knife stuck out from the enemy's chest. "I was about to tell them it would be another story."

"Grab their weapons. We need to move."

"Where to?"

"The rendezvous. Seaside Dale. Farm house with a swing in an old tree out front. North-west from the beach."

"That's was Brutus said?"

Ash heard the suspicion in Roy's ask. "That's what Brutus said."

"He's got a habit of getting his friends killed."

***

The beach was sodden. Progress was slow. They reached a field and expected to make better time from then on, but a marsh appeared before them. Each step sucked their feet down. Sea mist clung to the land. It was thin, but still played with their vision.

"What's that?" Roy pointed ahead.

A faint light swung back and forth rhythmically.

"Someone out walking early?" suggested Roy. "Country people do that."

"Or it could be our contact."

"The farm?"

Ash could hear Roy's breathing, and no doubt Roy could hear his. "Let's find out."

Both pulled themselves through the mire, and were close to exhaustion when they reached the perimeter of the farm. A low stone wall, collapsing with age, signalled the end of the bog. Ash rested his hands on the cold stones. They were a good eight-hundred metres away from the farm buildings.

Brutus's description of the place so far had been correct. They were north-west of the beach landing, and there stood an old tree, a swing hanging from a low branch.

The land sloped away. Timber was missing from the walls of a barn. The large door was open, angled awkwardly on its hinges. A gas lamp hung from a hook outside. It was still.

Ash gestured they move forward. Roy's footing tipped a stone in the wall to the ground. A thin layer of snow crunched underfoot. Weapons pointed left and right.

Ash moved to the barn, looked through the gaps in the walls. No movement. He listened for sound. Nothing. Then waved Roy to the other side of the door. The roof had failed its purpose a long time ago, with a line of splintered beams and loose planks being all that remained. The lamp's light filtered into the barn. Ash took one step inside.

The sound of a rifle being loaded came. "That's far enough!"

Ash sprang backward and around, keeping the wall of the barn to his back then crouched low. Roy had completed the same manoeuvre, then crept backwards further into the darkness away from the door, and found cover behind a trailer.

Ash's hesitation in firing the MP5 was sourced from believing that rifle would have blown a hole in his head by now if it was in the hands of an enemy.

"Who are you?" the voice inside demanded.

Ash nodded to Roy.

"You're waiting for Brutus, aren't you?" yelled Roy.

"You know, Brutus? Who are you?"

Ash crept further backward, seeking a hole in the walls to peer into the barn.

"Friends of Brutus. Something's happened. We need help," replied Roy.

"Put your guns down and then we can talk."

"No."

Ash spotted the man. He was no soldier. His finger rested on the trigger, and he held the weapon lazily.

Ash gestured to Roy. He tapped his weapon once and pointed to the ground.

"Alright," Ash called out. "We're trusting you."

He slipped the gun's sling from his shoulder, stepped to the barn entrance, and made an exaggerated show of putting the weapon down. Roy joined him, and copied his movements. They held their hands up high.

"I hope you know what you're doing," Roy whispered from clenched teeth.

A tall man walked out, shotgun pointed. He did not look much like a soldier, dressed in jeans, trainers and a thick woollen jumper under a raincoat.

"What happened to Brutus?"

"What's your name?" asked Ash, hands still overhead.

"Murray. And who are you?"

"Ash and Roy. We were ambushed on the beach. Brutus and the rest of our people were captured. We need help to get them back."

"Shit! I knew it. Something always goes wrong when he's involved."

"So we're talking about the same Brutus, then?" said Roy.

Murray lowered the shotgun. Ash and Roy lowered their hands.

"How many men do you have?" Ash asked.

"It's just me. All Brutus told me was to get a van, wait here and he would make contact. The lantern on the barn was the signal. I've been here for two days. Not seen a soul. Who has taken them?"

"We don't know." Ash offered Murray a handshake.

He took it. "Your name really Ash?"

"And I'm Roy." Roy picked up their weapons. "You've got a van?"

Murray nodded then pointed behind him. "It's parked to the back of the house, out of view. Brutus said he'd have men and equipment in need of transportation."

"You're not an operator then?"

"Do I look like one?"

Roy handed Ash his MP5. "You'll have to do."

Murray spat into the snow. "How many of them have Brutus?"

Roy shrugged. "More than fifteen? Couldn't tell for sure. But two less than they started with."

"What exactly are the three of us supposed to do? And don't say fight them trained killers."

"How many men can you scrape together in twenty-four hours?" Ash asked.

Murray rubbed at his forehead. "None. I work alone most of the time."

Ash looked around the farm. "Get the van started."

"And then?" said Murray, the shotgun moving left and right.

"Stop waving that rifle around," said Roy. "Someone could get hurt."

Murray disappeared behind the farmhouse. The van gurgled to life.

"I'm not dying to get Brutus back, Ash. I'm not scared to fight mind you, but I want to go home. If Brutus has walked us into a trap and there's not a better than average chance of us getting them all back, I'm walking away. You should do the same."

Ash could not fault Roy. Brutus spoke with a silver tongue. Promised wealth and protection from the coming pandemic. But he had led them into some sticky situations, and some Ash was none too proud of.

A long van bounced over the uneven land. It might have been white on another day, but now looked like a sepia photo. The side panels were scarred by rust. One headlight flickered with the bouncing. It was a piece of crap but then perhaps that was Brutus's plan. Who would suspect something so derelict to contain enough cash and guns to fund a small war?

"Come on!" shouted Murray.

Roy hauled himself into the passenger seat. Ash climbed into the back. There were no seats. He knelt and grabbed onto the headrest of the passenger seat.

"Kill the lights," ordered Roy.

Murray switched them off.

Roy pointed back over the marsh. "To the beach. And put your foot down. We're running out of time."

"We might want to head that way, but the road leads back inland. We'll double back later to get to the beach."

"You mean this thing doesn't fly?" asked Roy.

***

Brutus was blindfolded and bound with rope, his arms secured together above his head. The rope was attached to a chain which hung from the ceiling and kept him on his feet. He shook with the cold and cringed from the beating he received.

He remembered little. The floor was concrete and the smell of bleach overpowered anything else.

He pulled on the restraints and the chain rattled. Brutus opened and closed his mouth gingerly. It was stiff and swollen. His tongue played at a loose tooth. It would be out sooner rather than later.

He'd taken the risk and lost. Screwing with The Owls of Athena was a gamble. They'd slain many to ensure their secrets were not leaked, and no doubt Brutus and his men were next on the list of collateral.

Brutus shook the chain. Quick footsteps approached. A blow to the head staggered him but he could not fall. Something solid was pushed into his temple.

"You know what this is?"

"A little dick?"

It was pushed harder. "It's power and it's the instrument I'll use to end your miserable, pathetic existence." The accent was British.

"A small English dick then?"

9

"I've broken men tougher than you."

Something in the way he spoke suggested this to be personal. The pressure of the gun to his temple was gone. There should have been fear gripping Brutus right now, but instead, all he found was a numbness. He spent a lifetime inflicting this kind of torment on others. Deep down, he knew one day it would be his turn and he wouldn't walk away from it smoking a cigar. But Ash Gibbons and Roy Smart had not been captured. He did not know if they lived or died. He had to hope they'd made contact with Murray Jamieson. That was his only hope to get out of this alive.

A kick came to Brutus's stomach. Air burst from his lungs and he coughed and retched.

"I heard you were the toughest bastard out in the field. But here you are, spewing your guts up like a little bitch."

"Why don't you unchain me, and then we'll decide who the bitch is?"

Another blow, a hard fist to his face. There was a crack and his loose tooth snapped away. Brutus growled and spat. The tooth hit the floor.

"Where's my team?"

"How touching. Concern for the men you led down a path you barely understood. The Owls put a lot of trust in you, and you threw that aside."

"I didn't throw that aside. I outlived my usefulness. How long before you're next?"

"Brave words for a dead man, Brutus. As much as I'd like to simply pull the trigger now, I've been charged with getting certain information from you."

"I know nothing."

"Why did you come back to Britain? You could have gone anywhere in the world, found some stinking little corner, stayed off the radar but you came back here. Why?"

"You know with all the blows to the head, I can't quite remember."

The torturer gave a chuckle. "A damn comedian. Outstanding." He ripped off the blindfold. "I want you to see my face. I want you to know the person who is doing this to you."

One eye at a time opened, both blinking, both reluctant to open. But Brutus was keen to see who he would be killing as soon as the opportunity presented itself. The poorly lit room was small. No windows. Only one door. It reminded Brutus of a meat locker. The man collected a large boning knife from the lid of an oil drum.

"You look insipid," said Brutus. "Nothing to make me worry."

"Brave to be sarcastic in your position."

"Who are you?"

"Normally, I don't talk but with you it's different."

"Why?"

"I want you to know why you are suffering so."

"So this is personal?"

"The team you took out in the Sinai, you remember them, yes? They were my team."

"Your team, someone else's team, my father's team? It's all a job."

A punch to Brutus's right temple silenced him.

"It is not in my contract to kill you, Brutus." He ran the point of the knife down the length of Brutus's armpit.

"That tickles."

Another punch came to his left temple.

The knife pushed at Brutus's cheek. It pierced the skin.

"You give me the information we need and I'll hand your team over."

"We?"

"Only one of us is walking out of here, Brutus. I don't think your men will mourn you too long."

"Will your men mourn you?"

"Why did you come back to Britain?"

"Screw you."

The knife cut through his cheek and move down to his chin, running parallel to the scar already present. Brutus rocked at the pain. His captor grasped his face, turned his head and examined the wound.

11

"A touch deeper and I would have been able to see your teeth. Someone's already gone to town on your face. I'm giving you some nice symmetry."

Brutus sucked in a breath.

"I'll keep cutting you again and again until you speak. I'm in no rush and you have plenty of places I can practise my art."

The dull sounds of shouting came from beyond the door.

"Is that my men killing your men?"

"Still a comedian. I would suggest they are the sounds of my team having a little fun with your team. Perhaps they have been cut, just as you. Perhaps an eye has been taken out. Perhaps a finger has been sawn from a hand."

"I'm going to kill you."

"I'm growing impatient, Brutus. Answer my question or I'll slice off your balls."

The door to the room unlocked.

"I told you I didn't want to be disturbed!"

A pop sent his captor still, the sound echoing in the enclosed room. The knife fell from his hand. His knees buckled then his face slammed into the floor.

A balaclava-clad soldier moved into the room, his AK-9 trained on the fallen man. No markings on the uniform identified friend or foe. The AK-9 was a Russian-made rifle but that indicated nothing. Russia supplied arms globally. The soldier tugged at the restraints, let his rifle rest on the sling then pulled a knife from his belt and cut the rope that bonded Brutus's hands.

Brutus hit the floor hard. His arms numbed painfully. He lay there beside his captor, breathing hard. The round had passed through the centre of his captor's chest. He was bleeding out. In a few minutes he would be gone.

Brutus rolled to his stomach. The soldier left the room. The two men lay there, one dying and the other slowly recovering. Pain flushed through Brutus's joints, bringing them back to life. He moved his fingers, then his arms before finally being able to push himself upright. He leaned heavily on an oil barrel. The room rocked like a ship. He rubbed at his temple, swearing at the bursts of light that confused his vision.

Brutus recovered enough to take a few steps, bent down and snatched up the boning knife.

"That's the thing about power if it's over a country or a single person. It's transitional, fleeting. You just never know when you're luck will change. One minute you're at the top of the mountain." He used the blade to point toward the roof. "And the next, the next you're down, broken at the bottom. Did it even slip into your dull mind that it could end up like this? You bleeding out, me standing above you watching your last, agonising moments? Can you even talk?"

He did not reply, or could not.

"I'll let you into a little secret." Brutus knelt. "I've killed a lot of people. Women, men. Young and old. I don't really remember the number. That's not the secret though. Killing someone is the easiest thing in the world for me. It means as much as taking a piss. I almost enjoy the feeling, it breaks the monotony of life. You understand what I'm saying?"

The fingers on the captor's hands danced a slow movement.

"No matter how terrible I am or what horrors I've committed, it doesn't even begin to stack up against what's happening next. Have you seen the infected? Have you even seen what the Carrion Virus can do to a person? It changes them completely. Makes them strong. Reverts the poor bastards back to some primitive survival mode. I'd never seen anything like it."

Brutus leaned down closer to the dying man.

"I've seen how the world ends, my friend. It's not nuclear war, famine or goddamned aliens. The world will be murdered by the Carrion Virus. Count yourself lucky you won't be here to see it."

Brutus's picked up his tooth from the ground and rolled it between his index finger and thumb.

"You knocked my tooth out." His tongue slipped over the gap at his gum. "You know what? You can keep it."

With a backhand motion the blade slid across the dying man's throat. His eyes went wide, his lips mouthing silent words.

"Here," he said, pushing his tooth into the wound. "See you in hell, buddy."

Brutus stood with a groan at his protesting joints. He peered into the hallway. A team of four soldiers appeared casual, but to Brutus's trained eye, he could tell that was nothing more than an illusion.

"Are we alright, gentlemen?" he asked, and slowly bent, placing the knife on the ground.

One soldier pulled his balaclava off revealing a surprisingly boyish face; bright, blue eyes and a chin bare of stubble.

"Artyom sends his regards, Brutus," he said in heavily accented English.

Artyom Vetrov was a former KGB agent, who had retained links to his former employers. It was Artyom who arranged for Brutus to leave Egypt and return to Britain with weapons, cash and equipment. All he had asked for in exchange was a live subject infected with the Carrion Virus Stage Three. Brutus didn't much care what the Russian needed it for, only that it was a weighty currency. And the deal was done.

"The others?"

"Safe. Outside. And we found three in a van coming to your rescue." His smile was glib.

***

The soldiers led Brutus outside to a frigid morning. The sun promised to break through but it was still some time off. His escorts left him and quickly disappeared.

All members of Brutus's team were seated on the ground, Ash Gibbons and Roy Smart, too, along with a shaken Murray Jamison.

"What happened?" Ash snapped and stood, hands on hips.

"It would appear that The Owls of Athena's reach is longer than I thought. We need to move quickly, split up and disperse, keep our heads down for the next few weeks."

"Then what?"

"We wait."

"For what?" asked Ash.

"The end of the world," replied Brutus without the hint of a smile.

It was true in one sense, the world would end. Not outright, but the dynamics would change, and humankind would evolve into something unrecognisable.

"Sorry we're late," Brutus said to Murray. "Got tied up. That your van?"

Murray nodded. "It'll be a tight squeeze but we'll manage."

"Good. Help the lads in."

Brutus knew he had screwed up. He promised his men a lot and believed he could deliver. Safe passage back into the country, money, supplies and something worth more than money; a safe haven in the storm that was to come. He spoke with utter conviction and the men followed. He had underestimated The Owls of Athena. Brutus would not do that again.

Magnus Munson, Niall Campbell, Stuart Taylor and Freddo McLeod were still with them. Alive. It could have been different. And he needed them, needed all of them. He could not complete the remainder of his task alone.

CHAPTER 2

HEARTH AND HOME

Eric sat in his favourite armchair, feet propped up on the coffee table. It was Christmas.

His wife Jacqui wrapped in her dressing gown, scrapped butter onto toast in the kitchen and poured tea. In the lounge, his two children played with their new houseguest. Jane Appleby was a nurse Eric rescued from Aberdeen before the airport was bombed. Luke and Katie vied for her attention. Luke wanted Jane to taken notice of a blue train engine he held aloft. Katie wanted Jane to read books with her.

Jane's cough was easing, the antibiotics taking her from the brink of pneumonia. She was still too ill to return home, so Eric insisted she stayed. And Jacqui agreed. The kids loved Jane. Eric hoped being with his family helped her forget what happened. But then Eric wasn't sure anything much could achieve that.

Black Aquila had been disbanded after the Aberdeen debacle. Heavy losses and interference from the shadow group The Owls of Athena meant Eric was unemployed, sitting at home waiting for what happened next. His superior Ben Williamson promised some kind of covert retribution but Eric knew it to be hot words spoken in the moment of failure. It didn't stop Eric from being extra cautious. Three Glocks. One in the hallway in a locked drawer, one in the bedroom taped under the bedframe, one atop the kitchen cupboards. And when Eric was in Aberdeen, he instructed Jacqui to prepare to leave the house at a moment's notice. The bags were still packed.

Jacqui delivered two plates of toast and three mugs of tea to the coffee table like a seasoned waitress. Eric dropped his feet to the floor.

"Right, you two," Jacqui said to the kids, "time for bed. Say your goodnights."

The little protest got them nowhere so they hugged Jane and Eric before disappearing with their mother upstairs. Jane pushed herself from the floor, coughing with the movement and plonked onto the sofa. She sipped at the tea.

"Don't be shy. Eat some of the toast."

It became a ritual most nights for the three of them to sit and talk for an hour or so after the kids went to bed.

"I wish Jacqui would let me sort the tea from time to time."

"You're our guest. She wouldn't have it any other way. Besides, you're still sick. You need rest."

"That's all I've done. I don't want to put you out any more than I already have. So, I was thinking, maybe it's time for me to head back up north, try to make it home."

"Don't be silly," said Jacqui, returning to the room. She picked up her mug. "You're welcome here for as long as you want to stay."

"That's really very kind, Jacqui. I just think about everyone back home and feel like I should be there, doing something."

"You've done enough," said Jacqui. "It's time to let others take some responsibility."

Eric crunched toast and washed it down with tea. He knew that comment was meant for him, too.

"It's academic at the moment anyway," he said to Jane. "The weather's still bad, the worst in living memory and there's no transport between here and there. You're stuck here."

Travel in the UK had become difficult. Public transport for the most part was suspended. Businesses closed on government orders. It was as if the nation held a breath waiting for the next outbreak of the Carrion Virus. Eric knew the situation in Aberdeen had worsened since they left. The military presence had been pushed back from the gains already made. The threat of the infected meant that the policy was now extermination. Maybe it would be best to drop a bomb, erase the mistakes made and contain the virus in one hit.

"Eric, you're miles away." Jacqui watched him with a look of concern.

Eric mumbled an apology around his mug of tea. He did not like to talk about Aberdeen more than he had to. Jacqui was spooked enough. Eric masked as much as he could but lately his veneer slipped. An oppressive silence descended on the quiet room, only broken by the ticking of the clock and the crunch as Jane ate a piece of toast.

"Well," said Jacqui. "I think I'll head up to bed."

"I'll be up soon." Eric squeezed her hand.

"Goodnight," said Jane.

Jacqui was gone.

"What were you thinking about?" Jane asked.

"Nothing much."

"I keep thinking about all the people we lost. I see faces with no names. Hear voices with no faces. I can't get them out of my head."

"I know what you mean," he said solemnly.

"Eric? The virus won't be contained in Aberdeen, will it?"

"I don't know."

"You're lying," she snapped quietly. "With everything we've been through, don't think of me as an idiot."

"No." He placed his mug on the table. "I don't think it'll be possible to contain it in Aberdeen. There's been some isolated outbreaks elsewhere in Europe which were quickly contained."

"You once called the virus a weapon?"

"All the evidence points to a deliberate outbreak."

"Why Aberdeen?"

"What?"

"Why Aberdeen? If I wanted to infect a huge population, I'd pick a huge city. London maybe. Or Paris. Any outbreak there would be impossible to deal with."

It was a question Eric had pondered for some time. He stood and stretched. "I don't have an answer for you. Get some sleep, Jane. We'll talk more tomorrow."

Eric slipped into bed next to Jacqui. She was reading a tarnished paperback.

"Everything okay?" she asked.

"Sure." He kissed her on the cheek.

Why Aberdeen?

***

The stiff plastic of the hospital seat was unforgiving, but it had become Gemma Findlay's only option for a bed. The manic evacuation from Aberdeen had displaced many, and Gemma was deposited into a hospital thirty miles outside the Aberdeen exclusion zone. She had become the lost-looking woman who slept in the corridor under a thin hospital blanket, using a holdall full of cameras and equipment as a pillow. The slight curves of the seat disallowed any natural position in sleep, and the busyness of the place offered little opportunity to do that. Her fate could have been worse.

Gemma stood and twisted until she heard the *pop* in her back, then stretched some more. She shivered as she always did in the dim corridors. The weather outside was still cruel. It seemed like the Carrion Virus and the snowstorm went hand in hand, a kind of symbiotic relationship. Gemma knew better than to hope that when one disappeared, the other would follow. On the radio, the virus had been described as the greatest challenge facing the United Kingdom since the threat of invasion during the war. The surrealism of Aberdeen gave way to an unforgiving acceptance. This was how the world was now, the old never to return.

Gunfire ripped through the quiet of the clinical halls, and rang for seconds after. Gemma no longer recoiled from the sudden bursts. Nobody told her what the shots were, but she could hazard a pretty accurate guess. Those in Stage Three of the virus were being despatched. There was no other option. Those suffering the infection showed a strength beyond anything she had ever known, and their ability to spread the virus was lightning fast.

A door opened and a doctor stepped into the corridor. He pulled the stethoscope from his shoulders and let it drop to the floor. He wept quietly to himself, the only real sign he shed tears was the shaking of his shoulders.

Gemma made a move to comfort him.

He wiped his eyes. "I beg your pardon," he said, softly and retrieved his stethoscope before returning back to the room he came from.

Gemma angrily snapped off the Black Aquila badge clipped to her lapel. Not since Aberdeen had she seen anyone from Black Aquila. Ben Williamson had charged her to investigate the outbreak, find clues and leads to pursue. She achieved a measure of success, however, for all the progress she felt a million miles away from an actual breakthrough.

Why am I still here? I should be home with my family, safe. Who would miss me? I'm only in the way here. Another burst of gunfire and the expected resonance.

Gemma scooped up her bag. She had endured more than her fair share. Screw Ben Williamson. Screw Black Aquila. She was going home.

She rounded the corridor and spared a quick glance inside a treatment room. It was not a holding area for the infected. Those inside were being treated for conventional injuries. Seven beds were occupied and there was space for an eighth. The bed itself was missing. Surgery perhaps, or worse.

A soldier on patrol appeared at the doorway. "You can't be here. This is a restricted area. Go back now."

Gemma raised her hands and mumbled an apology.

The soldier followed her for a distance, his hand on his weapon at his side. Gemma assumed the soldiers in the hospital were not from regular units. The uniforms they wore were suitably nondescript; no rank or insignia. But they were both security and executioners.

Where the inner corridors were deserted for the most part, the vestibule of the facility buzzed with activity. Medical staff and troops worked around each other. A dozen different phones rang and too many voices mingled into a chorus. She stormed through the automatic doors.

The snow had stopped several hours before, the fall in the parking lot stomped into a mush. Military vehicles populated each space and beyond them, a series of barricades manned by a soldier and a machine gun. She pulled her coat tight anticipating a long journey ahead. It was still early evening but already night was falling.

"It's a cold night to be outdoors," said a voice from behind.

Gemma spun to the source, the sound so sudden it startled her.

A man clad in a thin hospital gown detached himself from the shadow of the doorway and approached. His gait showed he favoured his left foot. An IV line was attached to his right hand.

Gemma hid her surprise. "It's a cold night to be out when you should be in bed, I imagine."

The man laughed. "You have a point."

He was slightly older than Gemma, and stubble darkened his pale skin. Superficial wounds had almost healed on his face; scrapes and bruises as if he had fallen from a bike and landed heavily.

"I've seen you around the hospital these last few days. Always thought of saying hello but never did."

"That's great," said Gemma. "If you don't mind, I think I'll be going now. It'll be completely dark soon."

"You've not asked my name," said the man, a hint of a smile playing across his face.

Gemma disliked the gesture. "You're right. I didn't." She took the steps leading from the hospital. It only occurred to her then that there did not seem to be any traffic. Nor the sound of traffic. In fact, it was eerily quiet. The evening closed in with a seasonal speed.

"My name is Jacob and I'm going to let you in on a secret." He was uncomfortably close, enough that his breath tickled the back of Gemma's neck. "You can't go anywhere. You're too close to the outbreak. Travelling is by permit only. No public transport. Only the military runs buses between certain points. We're stuck here."

Gemma stopped and faced Jacob. "What's your problem? Are you trying to scare me? I've been through Aberdeen and seen all kinds of hell, so a creepy bastard like you is a walk in the park."

One of Jacob's eyebrows arched, and to Gemma's satisfaction his smile dropped away.

"I'm sorry, okay. I didn't mean to sound like I did."

"So what do you want?"

"Why do you think I want something? I'm just out here, taking some fresh air and happened across you."

It was Gemma's turn to smile. "Don't bullshit me. You want something so please, just come out and say it. Otherwise, this conversation is over."

Snow drifted down again. Jacob looked up into the darkening sky, but Gemma kept her eyes fixed on the creep, and knew he felt her stare to be boring holes of fire into his skull. Sometimes it surprised her how forceful she had become. Surviving hell does that to a person.

Jacob looked back to her. "Okay. I know you're with Black Aquila. I saw your badge on that coat. I can assume that you're here because you were rounded up and moved out of Aberdeen before security broke down. There's no way to get away from here, to wherever the hell you want to go. Not without a pass. And I don't think you or I are a priority when it comes to issuing them."

"And?"

"I want out of here as much as you. You're a woman of means, with connections. You can make it happen."

"Ah, there it is. I'm your ticket out of here. And what makes you think I would even dream of helping you?"

Jacob pulled the hospital gown tight, and rubbed his arms. "Two people tried to leave against the instruction of our military guardian angels. One was shot dead. The other was beaten so badly he's lying in a comma in ICU. The military are not here for our protection, they're here to prevent a further outbreak. And the gloves are off."

Two soldiers, balaclavas over their faces stepped past Gemma and Jacob giving them only a customary look.

"All this is very interesting," Gemma said, lowering her voice. "But you've not told me one important thing. Why do *I* need *you*? If I can call in a favour, why would I need to take you with me? I'm a little short on goodwill and charity these days."

The smile returned to Jacob's face. "Because you don't have a phone and I'm the only person who can get you access to one."

***

Gemma stamped her feet freeing them of snow. She wasn't pleased to be back at the hospital. She'd have to return to those uncomfortable seats. Jacob limped back to his room. He waved to Gemma, that unpleasant smile still plastered to his face. Gemma resisted the urge to flip him off. There was a lot she hated about Jacob after the fifteen minutes they had spent together. Actually, there was nothing redeeming about him. He was a user.

Gemma headed past the small waiting area and the disused café. The sounds were still chaotic. Phones rang with frantic regularity. Why were the phones ringing if you couldn't make any calls? It made it all the more frustrating. They rang. They rang some more. Some rang out. They buzzed inside her head. Why weren't they being answered? Gemma marched to the reception desk. The phone closest stopped its ringing. She picked up the receiver and punched 9 into the dial and waited. An automated error message played, informing her that the line accepted incoming calls exclusively before going dead.

"Hey! What do you think you're doing?" A receptionist, reached over from the next phone and pulled the receiver from her hand. "These are for emergencies only."

"I have an emergency. I want to make a call home."

"These lines only take incoming calls."

"But you're not answering them."

"We'll get to them when we can."

"I need to let my parents know I'm okay. Where can I make a call?"

Hoop earrings bobbed as the woman shook her head. Gemma spied a moment of compassion, or was it exhaustion? There was a lot of that going around.

"None of us can make calls out of here. Not at the moment. Now please, go away before you get us both into trouble."

That looked altered to fear. The woman feared for her own safety.

Gemma stepped away and studied the activity of the reception area. All operations were recorded via pen and paper. The three computer terminals that the receptionists would usually have used were pushed to the side, now redundant. Patient files were piled high behind the protective barrier and constantly being added to with each new call.

She craned her neck around a pillar to where the files were stored. Long, metal cabinets, with small locks in the centre of each drawer. Most had keys inserted into the locking mechanism. Jacob's file would be in there. There was no way for her to access it, not without both the receptionists and the patrolling soldiers seeing her.

Jacob was an unknown factor. He could have been trying to entrap her, looking for potential troublemakers to report to the military.

Oh how she wanted to be gone from that place. There was a way. She could call in a favour from Black Aquila. But a favour would need to be returned. That was how it worked. Nothing for free, and she was still technically on their payroll.

She returned to the discomfort of her plastic seat, pulled the thin blanket up to her shoulders and seethed.

***

Ryan Bannister followed Law's instructions, deliberate and methodical in every detail and every nuance. For the past two days Ryan walked the streets of Seattle, his hoodie pulled up high, and placed containers of the Carrion Virus around the city. It felt like he visited almost every mall, carefully sliding the canisters where nobody would see them. Beneath bins. Under vending machines. In central displays. In lockers and the dark spaces beneath elevators.

He headed to the next destination, sniffing heavily. The cold weather was playing havoc with his sinuses. His phone rang.

"Yes?"

Law spoke in hushed tones. "Your next target is the Seattle Central Library. Three canisters. Understand?"

"Yes, I understand."

The phone clicked dead. Ryan wiped the screen free of the raindrops and searched on Google for the fastest route. He was just off 8th Avenue, the walk would take a little over ten minutes, perhaps nine if he wanted to raise a slight sweat. Ryan moved through the park, his pace keen, his eyes watching for people watching him.

Up ahead, police and ETMs and paramedics stood over a figure on the ground. Some leaned over the body. Some stood with hands on hips. Some were more casual, perhaps bored, perhaps keen to be elsewhere having a bite to eat or a coffee to heat up their hands. He spied arms and legs at awkward angles, and assumed the prognosis was not positive. He'd skirt around, avoid being noticed by people who were good at noticing things. He adjusted his backpack with little care. Carrying lethal cargo on his back no longer filled him with dread. A helicopter hovered overhead. Ryan looked up. For a moment he considered that Law would be perched above, observing everything through a high-powered rifle.

Those bored police officers formed a line, moving outward from where the medical staff worked pushing back the inevitable circle of voyeurs. His phone rang.

"Hello?" he said, after the wash of static faded from the encryption.

"You're late," said Law with his usual bluntness.

"I don't know the area."

"Go to the park bench, fifteen steps ahead. Go now."

"Are you in the helicopter?"

"You read too much fiction."

Ryan reached the bench just as rain started to fall. "And what am I doing here?"

"The trash can next to it, one of our canisters is in it. Retrieve it now before the cops reach you. Do it now."

The officers were pushing the onlookers further outward, and closer to Ryan. He stuffed his phone into his pocket, stood between the bin and the crawling crowd, reached in, pushed aside a damp newspaper, and met with something sticky that he did not want to think about. Then his hand found the cold exterior of the canister and pulled it free. He stepped away from the bin, stuffed the canister into his backpack, and looked up to the helicopter. Was it going to follow him? Perhaps Law was in it after all. Ryan moved off away from the police and their crime scene, turned a sharp right and stood beneath the wide arms of a tree. His phone rang.

"I've got it."

"I can see that."

"You are in the helicopter." He moved from the shelter of the tree and looked up to the sky.

"Consider me everywhere if it makes you happy, Ryan."

"Then why didn't you get the package yourself?"

"You're not understanding the bigger picture, and you've failed to comprehend the key question."

"What question?"

"Why is one of our packages in a trash can not a stone's throw away from a dead man?"

"And this is where you don't tell me, right?"

"Actually, I will tell you. The dead man was one of our deliverers. He decided to ignore the calls on his phone and he ditched the package. He became a risk. But he won't be talking now."

"So what? This is a warning to me?"

"Exactly. You've been given some privilege, don't abuse it."

"And this happens with all of your deliverers? There must be thousands of them."

"Yes. And everyone is watched, everyone is accounted for."

"How? How is that possible?"

"You've another delivery to make."

"I know. The library."

"Remember, Ryan, you're being watched, always."

The line went dead. The rain fell heavier. Ryan pinched the hoodie tight to his chin. The rain washed the city's sidewalks. He wondered how many of the Carrion Virus canisters had been placed around the city. He wondered how many deliverers had been killed. Not too many, he decided, otherwise he would have been ordered to collect discarded canisters more often, wouldn't he? More to the point, when were the planted canisters scheduled to release their deadly contents?

CHAPTER 3

THE WINTER OF ALL DEAD SOULS

Eric touched his constant companion concealed beneath his coat. He never ventured anywhere without his Glock. The supermarket was quiet. It certainly had customers, but conversation did not exist. The minimal fruit and vegetables were past their best. He grabbed a bunch of blackened bananas and three soft oranges, scooped up a basket and moved on. There were more *Out Of Stock* signs than price tags.

Staff wore latex gloves, disposable aprons and facemasks. Shoppers kept their eyes down. One woman walked about with a scarf over her face, her hand pushing it tight as if it were some kind of respirator. How many wandering the aisles were destined to suffer the virus? Did they truly know what was coming? The reports coming out of Aberdeen were vague, but enough to bring real fear. Eric knew more than a hundred-thousand people were dead, but the government held tight to that information.

Eric grabbed teabags, tinned fruit salad and tinned fish, bandages, cereal, biscuits, tinned peas and beetroot. As much as he could carry to the checkout, and grabbed chocolate from the counter. His kids would smile when they saw his last purchase.

The assistant was a boy, not a man. There was no managerial staff to be seen. Eric let out a gruff laugh.

The boy looked at him, the mask burying any expression, but Eric could guess.

"Sorry," said Eric. "Laughter isn't heard much these days I suppose."

Eric left the store, three bags cutting into his hands. His mobile rang. He dropped one of the bags and pulled the phone free from his pocket. The number withheld, he answered. "Eric Mann."

"Good to hear your voice. It's Ben. I'll be at your house in thirty. You home?"

"I'll be there."

Eric looked back at the supermarket, to those faces looking anywhere but up. The woman with the scarf scurried to a car. It was a new model. She had money, but that wouldn't save her. If Ben Williamson was making a personal visit it could only mean one thing.

***

The ward was dark with the only light slipping along the floors from the nurses' station. The male nurse behind the desk slept, his chin tucked into his chest. If one of the patrolling soldiers found him that way, he'd be in for a loud reprimand.

Gemma could not sleep, her mind fiddling with a hundred ideas and scenarios. Jacob made an offer but gave no more than a vague promise. Perhaps it was her journalistic nature that fuelled her quest to know more. Or perhaps she just wanted a way out, and soon.

She drew the curtain around Jacob's bed. He was asleep, no smile on his face, his jaw fallen, his tongue moving with every inward breath. The sound of the curtain on the rail seemed impossibly loud but he did not stir. Probably all drugged up.

Gemma perched on the visitor's seat next to the bed. For the briefest of moments she considered grabbing the IV line and yanking it free. Too much blood and too risky. He'd surely send a thunder of noise to the air. She shook his shoulder, lightly at first then with more insistence when he didn't respond.

Jacob opened his eyes, the serenity of his medicated sleep dropping away. A panic struck him, his eyes went wide. Gemma slapped a hand over his mouth.

"Shut up," she hissed into his ear. "Calm down and shut up. Blink if you understand."

Jacob blinked.

"I'm going to take my hand away. If you call out I'll hurt you, do you understand?"

He tried to mumble something from under her hand. She frowned at his stupidity, and clamped down on his mouth harder.

"If you understand blink once. Now."

Jacob blinked. Gemma removed her hand. He simply stared.

"You can talk now."

"What the hell are you doing?" He tried to sit up.

"You offered me a deal and I want to accept it, on one condition."

"What's that?"

"You answer all my questions."

Even in the dark of the ward, the churning of that question in his mind was telling on his face.

"And if I refuse?"

Gemma pushed him back down onto his pillow. "You think you're the only person in this hospital with access to a satellite phone? It wouldn't be too difficult to convince a doctor or a soldier to do me a favour. So, you see, Jacob, you came to me with an offer and the reality is, I don't need you."

"Then why are you here?"

"Because there's more to you than you let on. You know something and it's important. I don't know what or why, but you do. I'll get to the bottom of it or if I don't, I'll leave you here to rot. Funny thing about Aberdeen, for all the cutting edge technology they still couldn't contain the virus. How long do you think a piece of shit backwater hospital like this has? A week or two? You'll be one of them, or dead. Either way, I won't care. I'll be gone. You came to me with a deal." She shook her head. "Now I'm coming to you with a final chance."

Gemma squeezed his hand where the IV needle pierced his vein. Jacob sucked in air.

"Tomorrow morning. I'll expect an answer. Sleep well, Jacob. I know I will."

She left his bedside without looking back. In the corridor she braced herself against the wall, her arms and legs shaking.

***

A hand shook her awake. Gemma sat bolt upright, grabbed for the thin-bladed knife tucked into her boot.

"Easy, it's me. Jacob."

"What are you doing here?"

His eyes focused on the knife. "I want to talk to you, and since you so rudely interrupted my sleep I thought I would return the favour."

"This isn't a game, Jacob. You mess with the wrong person and you're dead. There's no coming back from that. Dead, or worse."

"You wanted an answer by morning. I'm going to give you an answer now. Everything. Honestly. I need to get out of this place. The hospital is dying, everyone in it just doesn't realise it yet. Each day you notice a staff member absent, and patients go missing, too. Each day you wonder if they succumbed to the virus or if the soldiers got them. I can't leave on my own." Jacob pointed to the knife. He smiled, but it was not full of sarcasm, nor was it friendly. There was fear, an admission that the dynamics of his confidence had changed. "You don't need that. Please, put it down."

She returned the weapon to her boot.

"Where did you get that thing?"

"From a friend." She sat up.

"May I?" he asked, indicating a seat one away from her.

"I'm going to sit here and listen, and you're going to talk." She pulled her memo recorder from the camera bag, and clicked it on.

"What's that for? I didn't agree to that."

"Insurance. You can start talking when you want."

Jacob licked his lips, kept his eyes down at his hands.

"We can trust each other, Gemma. I'm sorry how I was before. I haven't been acting the way I should. It's this godforsaken place. It's insane and I couldn't see a way out. With you I … I acted badly." He blew out his cheeks. "I don't know where to start. I guess I'll tell you my history and how I came to be here. I work in construction, or I did. I'll probably never work in the industry again. We'd been working onsite in Glasgow for almost eighteen months. I'd moved up from

Cornwall for this job. I was the project manager. It was a new build, down on the Clyde side. Eighteen storeys, a high rise. I won't bore you with the details. This wasn't a typical build for the UK, not outside of London anyway. It dominates the skyline. Like I said, not typical. The construction was pretty much complete, the electronics and final clean-up were underway. Another team of workers came in to complete it. Now, it's standard for me and a few of the others to be there and sign off at the end. Some suits and ties arrived and told us to ship out, down tools and leave. I was straight on the phone to the company. They said the same. Stop whatever you're doing and get the hell off site."

Jacob wiped his forehead with the back of his hand.

"The entire construction team left. I stayed behind. I poked into business that wasn't mine to pry into. The security detail caught me. They beat me so bad I couldn't walk properly for a week. I crawled out to the roadside in the snow and someone called an ambulance. Next thing I knew, I'm here and the world has turned to shit."

"No police?"

Jacob shrugged. "I was waiting for them to come but nobody ever did. I guess there were more important things happening than some guy being beaten up in Glasgow."

"The building you worked on, what was its purpose? Residential? Business?"

"The building was neutral. It had extensive underground vaults. Possibly for storage or perhaps power generation. We build to a specific design but it could have been anything from offices to retail space. All I know is somebody didn't want me knowing any more about the building than I had to."

"And you think it's somehow linked to the outbreak?"

Jacob shook his head. "I don't know. And I don't want to know. Trying to find out almost got me killed. One thing that had come up was the word Athena. I don't know the relevance, or if there is any."

Gemma switched off the memo recorder, tidied her hair and ran her tongue over her teeth. "I think you and I can do business."

"I want to get out of here, get my family and find somewhere to lie low until it all blows over."

"You have access to a satellite phone. How?"

"Leave that to me. You'll get us both out of here?"

"If I can. It might take some doing. I've become a little less useful lately but I think I still have enough friends to do the job."

"And you can get us both out?"

"If I can get myself out I can get you out, too."

"Promise?"

"What, you want a Girl Guides pinkie promise?"

Jacob grinned with a softness, probably the most genuine expression he had shown. "I'll work on the satellite phone. You should be ready to leave."

Gemma patted her bag. "Everything I have is here."

***

The drive home was slow and frustrating. Several checkpoints had been set up manned by both police and military. Eric stepped out of his car as instructed. A medical technician checked his pulse, squeezing his wrist. She nodded, satisfied. Eric was ordered to tilt his head and allow her to take his temperature, the thermometer placed just inside his ear. It beeped several times before revealing a normal reading. She shone a short torch into his eyes, and swung it left to right, before turning her back to him.

"So I'm not infected?" Eric asked with a dull tone, then rubbed at the white blotches distorting his vision.

She did not answer, and went about prepping for the next motorist who had been stopped.

A field tent had been pitched off the road. Eric was certain others would be subjected to more in-depth questioning and examination in that tent, those unlucky enough to display anything but absolute normal readings on the basic tests.

"The purpose of your journey?" asked another office.

"I'm returning home with shopping for the family."

The officer checked inside the car. "You may go."

"How many do you have in the tent?"

"You may go," the officer repeated, and waved him on.

Eric headed home. Jacqui's face appeared between the curtains as he pulled into the drive. Seconds later, she rushed from the house.

"Where have you been? We were worried sick."

"Why? What's happened?"

"I've been trying to call you. It just beeped and went dead. I … I thought something had happened."

Eric pulled Jacqui close. She did not cry, but trembled in his arms. Jacqui's resilience was faltering more each day. He couldn't blame her.

"I was only gone a short time."

"I know, but …"

"I'm sorry. The signal has been dropping out a lot lately." He kissed her lightly on the head. "I have chocolate for the kids."

A tired smile appeared. "They'll love it."

"Is anyone here?"

"No, why? Are you expecting someone?"

"Maybe. Let's get you indoors."

"Did you buy anything other than chocolate?"

"Of course. You ask, and I do." He swatted her playfully on her behind. "Stick the kettle on. I'll bring the shopping in."

"Coffee or tea?" she called from the door.

"Coffee. Hot."

He grabbed the bags and closed the door with a foot.

A black Audi with tinted windows pulled up.

"Never thought I'd see the day shopping bags were a burden to Eric Mann."

"Carter. You Ben's bodyguard now?" Carter was an operative for Black Aquila, and fought with Eric in Aberdeen and a half-dozen times in different warzones around the globe.

"Just keeping busy. He's finishing off some calls in the car."

Eric moved the bags to his left hand. The two men shook hands.

"Good to see you."

"We'll see."

"You know why he called me?"

"No, but things are heading toward hell out there."

They both looked to the house. Jacqui's expression was a mixture of alarm and determination and acceptance. She knew the signs. She knew Eric's work. And she knew he was needed.

"She'll be pissed," Carter said low.

"Yes, she will."

"Well don't just stand there," called Jacqui, her voice pleasant, but no smile reached her lips. "Come in and get warm. The kettle's on."

Two men climbed from the car, one opening the back door. Ben Williamson unwound from the seat, a black scarf around his neck.

***

Williamson had aged half a decade in three months. Deep, black circles clung beneath his eyes. His lips were cracked and dry. Drinking too much of the wrong stuff. He looked like a dehydrated insomniac.

Eric's fingers tapped at the table, waiting for Ben Williamson to start.

Williamson spread his hands. "Events have moved rapidly, Eric. To the point that I believe we are on the precipice of a world changing event. I'm no longer involved in any operational matters. I've been left out in the cold. I still have a few sources who will trickle information my way, but it's not been enough. Not near enough. We know of The Owls of Athena and something called The Athena Protocol."

"Which is?" Eric stilled his fingers.

"We don't know, but this group has resources beyond our wildest dreams. Someone's helping them. They can't operate without the compliance of governments. Or at least part of."

"You know this for a fact?"

"No. My theory is that The Athena Protocol is the beginning of the new phase of their operation. Aberdeen was the first phase, almost a combat test, and this new protocol is phase two."

"The situation in Aberdeen has gone to hell," said Carter. "Reports are hard to come by but after the destruction of the airport, the military surged their numbers. Containment was not considered after the airport. Unofficial projects resulted in a sixty to seventy percent casualty rate."

"Christ. Out of what? Two-hundred-thousand?"

"Give or take." Carter sipped his tea.

"So this second phase I imagine will be to hit another city," added Williamson.

"In the UK?" asked Eric.

Williamson shrugged. "We don't know. If we knew their aims then we could assume a little more. Perhaps they're attempting to destabilise the United Kingdom. Perhaps they're seeking the recall of foreign military assets. Or perhaps they have another city in another country in their sights."

"If the Carrion Virus took hold in London, we would never be able to contain it. I don't get it," said Eric. "What do The Owls of Athena get out of this? What's their goal? People don't act without a purpose."

"They're purpose is to release the virus," offered Carter.

"I understand that, but why? What do they get out of it?"

Nobody had an answer. All three men spent time in quiet, the clock ticking faithfully in the lounge.

"I suppose that's what we need to find out. What is the end result of all this?" asked Eric.

"That isn't something we can answer at the moment. We simply don't know, or have enough to make an educated guess. But you'll notice things are changing here. Road blocks, random checks. The military are patrolling in many cities. They're guarding key buildings. Large gatherings are broken up by police. Britain is grinding to a halt. It's like the nation is holding its breath. What comes next won't be good, Eric."

"So why are you here? You're bringing tidings of fear and death but what's your purpose?"

Williamson drained his drink, and placed the mug back to the table.

"Gemma Findlay. You remember her? Of course you do."

"Of course," said Eric. "I wondered what happened to her after Aberdeen fell."

"She got out, evacuated with some army units, and now she's in a decanting hospital outside the city. She swindled a satellite phone, so now we have unauthorised contact with someone in the middle of it all, and she has information about a building The Owls of Athena are using."

"The source?" asked Eric.

"One of the patients in the hospital supposedly worked on the construction."

"A patient? An infected?"

"No. Not infected. She wants to cut a deal before she tells us more. We pull her out and she gives us the location."

"And you want me to go and get her?" said Eric after an impossibly long time.

"I'm not telling you that you have to go. I'm not even suggesting that you should go."

"Is she in danger?"

"Almost certainly," said Williamson. "If Aberdeen has taught us anything, it's that this outbreak is deadly even under controlled situations."

"If I accept how would I get there?"

"Fly some of the way, drive the rest. But it's not like you could just walk up to the gates and ask for her. It's a controlled military facility. You couldn't go in hard either."

"My family needs me."

"Carter will remain here if you wish him to."

Williamson presented the option to Eric as if he were neutral, with no preference, no bias. He was a sly bastard. He would likely be chewing at the bit to get the location of that building but knew that if he ordered Eric to go, he would resist.

"Carter?" said Eric.

"You know I'll protect them as if they were my own."

Eric knew the sincerity behind that promise.

"And you, Ben? What will you do now that things are going to hell?"

"I have a boat. I'm heading offshore until we can gauge how the land lies. If I'm wrong then I'll return and rebuild what's left of Black Aquila. If I'm right, then we'll head for safer waters."

"So you're running while we do the hard work?"

Williamson stood, an action that caused his stomach to rock the table. The mugs rattled.

"I don't need to remind you that you are an employee, Eric. I called you here as a mark of respect not to be accused of apathy. There's a hundred men on my roster who could serve me just as well." Williamson raised a finger. "There's a day coming you'll realise how lucky you are to have my generosity. Carter will remain here pending your decision. Say goodbye to Jacqui for me." Williamson left the house.

Carter hefted a holdall onto the kitchen table. "He's furious."

Eric unzipped the bag. "He's holidaying on a boat? He could have taken us all with him. Bastard."

Inside the bag were two AR-15 rifles, with several hundred rounds of ammunition, some silencers and tactical flashlights.

"Eric, don't be too quick to judge. No good pissing off the one man who can help."

"Help who?"

"The world. If you go get her, your family will be safe with me."

"I know, and Gemma's risked a lot. She needs help."

Carter zipped the bag closed. "She knew the danger before she got into this mess."

"What would you do?" Eric looked up to his good friend.

"Not for me to say. But if everything goes to plan, you could be back in a couple of days."

"When does anything ever go to plan?"

***

Five days! The way the situation was slipping at the hospital, Gemma was not sure there was five days left. She tapped the satellite phone against the cubicle wall. They made no promises but advised if they could help, it may take five days.

Five days!

She gave a final tap against the wall with the phone, flushed the toilet and left the bathroom. Jacob waited nervously peering around the corner and down the hallway.

"Well?" he demanded, holding out his hand for the phone. "You've been gone a long time."

She reluctantly handed it over. It would be handy to hold onto, have access to communications at almost any time, but she had an agreement with the creep, and it would do no good to alienate him. Not yet anyway. He put himself in considerable risk to acquire the phone. Using his silver tongue to access a part of the hospital he shouldn't have been able to, and then sneaking around to steal the phone.

"They're sending people to get us out of here," she lied. "They couldn't tell me exactly when, and since we're not contactable for the moment it could be anytime within the next five days."

"Five days?" Jacob half shouted. "Do they know how bad it is here? Maybe I should speak to them."

Gemma grabbed Jacob by the lapels of his dressing gown and backed him into the wall. "Listen. If you want to get out of here alive, you need to keep your head. You start talking to those people, we're dead. You start getting careless, we're dead. I can get you out of here, but you need to do what I say. You understand?"

Jacob pointed into her face. "You just make sure that you hold up your end of the bargain. You get me out of here and nothing bad will happen." He looked down the corridor beyond Gemma. "I'm not dying in this shithole."

If no rescue came within three days from Black Aquila, Gemma would make her own escape. Jacob could be goaded to making a rash move, she was sure. It would likely end with him being killed but that was the price of survival.

CHAPTER 4

WATCHER, WHAT DID YOU SEE?

Brutus sat in the van, the window down, his arm outstretched catching the drizzle that fell. The air was frigid and the rain freezing, but whilst sitting inside the van he found a comfortable compromise.

Brutus had driven up to Glasgow and had been watching The Owls of Athena's building for the last two days, sleeping in the back of the van when he needed. He was still a few streets away, by the river Clyde, but close enough to observe without arousing suspicion.

Brutus revealed his plans to nobody. He sent the rest of his team home to their families with orders to have them ready to travel. Families were a hindrance; they created priorities. That's why Brutus kept himself free of such anchors. But he recognised the priority of family was essential to his ambition for the future. His men would fight harder if they knew their families depended on that, and hard fighting was sure to come. His plan was to battle a shadow organisation with seemingly unlimited resources and zero accountability. And the odds of winning? He never cared for odds. If he paused to consider, he'd find them stacked against him.

In the two days since arriving he detailed on a notebook all vehicles that arrived and left. There were regular arrivals, small trucks and a few buses. The occasional construction vehicle came, and left soon after. A high wall surrounded the building, a manned gate barring entry into the compound. Beyond, the building looked out of place, architecture from America or China suddenly landing in the Scottish city. It was tall, a dark hue in colour, and in the dullness of the day appeared almost obsidian. At the summit, a helicopter pad.

The river ran so close to the wall, Brutus assumed some kind of protected marina existed. Smart, he admitted. If the roads were impassable then the building would make use of air and waterways. It was a building designed to outlast the coming catastrophe.

And Brutus wanted it.

But how to gain entry?

The drone of an aircraft engine thundered overhead. Brutus leaned out the window, gazed up to the grey skies. A helicopter gunship, an Apache raced overhead. He wiped the rain from his face. It was almost inconceivable that they would be flying over a British city. He chuckled at the thought.

He pushed open the door and stepped out. The rain fell heavier. His shoulders felt the cold. He walked to the river's edge and took a piss. Nobody was about. Nobody cared. Glasgow, like many other cities in the UK had almost ground to a halt.

An old pram lay abandoned a little to his right. It had been exposed to the elements for a time, the cover with tears, the wire frame rusted. A thought struck him. A way to enter the building. It was risky, and relied causing fear to another human. He excelled at that skill.

Brutus finished his piss, redressed himself then dug his ankles into the mud, pulled the pram from the stink and hauled it up to the street. He gave the contraption a kick to make sure no river rats remained. Nothing scuttled out. One wheel was slightly buckled. It would do as a prop.

It would be dark in a few hours. Brutus had enough time to grab something hot to eat before he enacted his new plan.

***

Night fell quickly. The rain stopped but the stench of a storm lingered. Brutus knelt between two abandoned cars, their windows smashed long ago. The old pram, now soaked in petrol, lay next to him, his lighter doing somersaults as his fingers flicked it around and around. Down the street, the lonesome glow of headlights appeared. A most welcome sight. He waited for the truck to approach closer, flicked his lighter into life, and tossed it into the pram. The cover caught with an ardent burst of light.

Brutus shielded his face from the heat, rocked back to his feet, then kicked the pram onto the road. The truck's brakes screeched. The pram was hit and tumbled over and over.

Brutus moved keeping low and using the cars as cover.

The driver jumped out. Brutus came from behind, threw a sharp elbow to the back of the neck. The driver stumbled forward. Brutus grabbed him by the back of his reflective coat, pulled his Glock out and pushed the barrel into the driver's neck.

"Do what I say and you don't die. Get back into the cab."

Brutus dragged him backward and they both entered the cab. He manoeuvred himself over to the passenger seat, keeping the weapon trained.

"Please, please. Take what you want."

"I'm not here for what you're carrying. Close the door and start driving. Slow."

The driver, a fat, balding man of advancing years turned to Brutus, opened his mouth but said nothing. He put the truck into gear and accelerated.

"I'm going to talk. You're going to listen. If you do everything I ask, you're going to live another day. Understand? Don't speak unless I ask you to."

He nodded.

"I'm not here for you, I don't care who you are. All I need is to get into the site you're heading to. Killing you means nothing to me. Get me in there and you go back to your life and this will seem just a nightmare."

He nodded again.

"What kind of security are they boasting?"

"Security cameras. A manned gate. Sentries on the wall. That's all I've seen when making deliveries."

"What checks do they do when you get to the gate?"

"A quick inspection of the rig and they check the paperwork and my ID." He turned to Brutus. "Please don't make me do this. Just let me go and you can drive in."

"Shut up." Brutus pushed the barrel of the Glock into the driver's cheek. "We're nearing the building. Do as you'd normally do."

Brutus manoeuvred himself behind the seats and into the sleeping compartment directly behind the driver. He pulled the curtain closed leaving enough gap to see the driver clearly.

The truck slowed and the driver lowered the window.

"ID please. And open the door."

The driver opened his door, pushing it out wide and handed over his ID badge.

"Everything alright tonight?" asked the guard, shinning his flashlight around the cab.

"Of course," said the driver. "It's been a long ride."

The guard looked between the ID and the driver's face. He nodded, handing back the badge. "Make your way inside."

The truck was again moving.

"Tell me what you see," whispered Brutus.

"Another wagon is about to leave the yard. There's a crew waiting to unload. Four men and a forklift driver. A guard is standing up on the loading bay. He's armed with a rifle or something."

"Pull up like normal. Keep everything as it should be. What are they wearing?"

"Safety gear."

"Like the coat on the peg back here?"

"Pretty much."

"How much freedom are you given when they're dealing with unloading?"

"We generally don't go far. Stretch the legs sort of thing. It takes about thirty minutes for them to unload me, then I'll be on my way back to the depot."

"You and I are going for a walk. Remember, I—"

"You don't want to kill me, but you will if you have to. Trust me, I just want to get home."

He backed the truck into the loading bay. The cargo door opened with a rattle, and the forklift moved with a warning rhythm of beeps.

"Get out, walk around the cab, meet me on the far side." Brutus pulled the coat on and slipped out the door, closing it quietly behind him. The forecourt was a choking haze of exhaust fumes. Men went about their tasks, shouting to one another. There was enough activity and dark recesses in the yard to provide suitable cover. For the moment, nobody questioned their presence. Together, they moved across the yard. They reached the inside of the building, a maintenance stairwell.

"Stay close." Brutus scanned for security cameras. None.

Cobwebs made patterns in corners. Dust suggested the stairs were rarely used. A cupboard nestled out of view behind the first stairwell. Brutus pulled the double doors open. Empty.

"What are you doing?" asked the driver.

"Did I ask you to speak?"

An idea formed so quickly, that Brutus acted without weighing up options. He seized the driver by the throat, spun him around, locked his arm around his neck and placed his free hand over his mouth. Brutus heaved back, lifting the man from his feet. Brutus put all his strength into squeezing the life from him. He weakly grabbed at Brutus's arms and face but could not find purchase. His arms slipped slowly down and his body became limp. A final rattle gurgled up from deep within him. Brutus dropped him to the floor. He chanced a quick glance back out the door to make sure the brief struggle had not aroused suspicion. Nobody came.

In the moment he found the cupboard stairs, he discovered his way back out of the sanctuary. He would spend the next half hour scouring the building then return to the lorry and drive it out. Or if there were extensive security checks before leaving he'd simply scale the wall.

***

Eric and Carter sat around the kitchen table, everyone else in the house was in bed.

"Carter, I need to talk about something with you."

"Go on."

"If I'm delayed and things here get worse I want you to look after my family until I get back."

Carter chuckled a little. "Ever the pessimist, Eric? You know you don't need to ask me."

Eric looked around the room, tapping a finger at the table. "If the infection hits, staying here isn't going to work. We need somewhere defendable and isolated."

Carter scratched his chin, then snapped his fingers. "I've got it," he said. "One of the company's clients is building an impressive rural home out in the sticks. It's about a three-hour drive from here. I provided some personal security for him and his family before all this happened."

"They wouldn't be at home?"

Carter shook his head. "They were living out of the country and this was a holiday home for when they came back. It might not be fully constructed but it'll offer shelter and some breathing room when we need it. I'll get the address and mark it on your map."

"Good. I'll get Jacqui to pack essentials in the car. Food, water and blankets. The camping supplies we have, too. Should the worst happen, we'll be ready."

"It's going to be fine," said Carter.

"Yeah," Eric said not believing himself.

Fourteen hours later Eric was in the air, rocking back and forth in the Chinook. The last time he rode in one, they were fleeing Aberdeen, watching destruction rain down on Aberdeen Airport. Then, it was crammed full of last minute refugees. Now, Eric was the only passenger, the crew his only company. He was strapped down, his weapon between his legs, barrel down.

The flight bounced, the aircraft rocked violently. Eric grasped the rails to his side. Flying was never something he relished. Eric's mind raced with a constant miasma of second guessing and regrets. Carter was more than capable, and Eric had left him more than half of the ammunition. Jacqui. His kids. Jane. He would not stop worrying until he returned home and saw for himself that all were safe.

The Chinook gave another lurch downwards. The pressure made his spine feel like it might push through his skin and rip at the seat. It levelled. Out the window the far north winter still held an iron grip, the land blanketed by white. Eric could not be sure, but it felt like they were losing altitude. The crewman at the hatch said instructions to Eric, but they were stolen away by the noise of the engines. The crewman tapped his headset twice, then pointed to Eric. *Headset!* He found a set hanging to his left and reached out.

The Chinook dropped, sudden and violent. The crewman at the hatch was thrown from his feet, his harness being the only thing to stop him from being bounced around the interior like a ball. Eric grabbed the rails, his knees squeezed tight holding the gun.

The aircraft was going down. The crewman shouted more words, but none could be heard.

Fear. Panic and thoughts of his family. Eric closed his eyes. He mouthed words of pleading, not to any God or any power.

The engines screeched. Thick black smoke filtered into the compartment. Burn to death, or be smashed into the ground? Don't be scared, he urged himself. You'll survive. Jacqui and the kids need you. Don't be scared.

The world exploded and Eric fell into a void.

***

Ryan Bannister was being followed. Someone behind was matching his steps. When he slowed, they slowed. He was scared and did all he could to stop himself from breaking into a run. It was that flight or fight response thing threatening to overtake his decision-making process.

Stay in public view. They won't touch you when there're people about.

He hoped he was right.

He kept to the sidewalks where people huddled under umbrellas. He stopped at a coffee stall, the rain tapping on a narrow canopy. He ordered whatever was first on the board. Ryan fumbled for a few soggy bucks in his pocket and handed them over. His hands shook. He added sugar to the coffee, trying to look casual and lazy. It was too much. He hated sugar in his coffee. It gave him horrendous migraines. *Stop shaking!*

People continued to make their way under umbrellas, their heads unseen, their gait quick. Women stood to his left, enjoying hot beverages. He wondered how many sugars they had. One woman was quite hefty, so he decided she took two sugars and drank at least a dozen cups each day, possibly accompanying each with an almond biscuit or a slice of poppy seed cake. He looked to the display of sweets: iced donuts, banana cake, cream-filled lamingtons, choc-chipped muffins in concertinaed, paper holders. There were no sweets sitting on a plate before the hefty lady. She must have scoffed hers down smartly before a companion asked to share. A couple kissed below a streetlamp, uncaring of the rain saturating their clothing. They kissed passionately. Their relationship must have been new and fresh, perhaps adulterous. Yes, he decided, those two were enjoying an extramarital affair. What would they say to their respective partners about their drenched clothing when they returned home? Perhaps they weren't returning home this day. Perhaps they were booked into a hotel close by, a cheap place with gaudy wallpaper and faded towels. Why weren't they there now instead of getting wet?

"Hey, buddy! Your change," said the vendor, holding out his hand.

"Oh, thank you," he mumbled, and reached across. He bumped one of the women and apologised profusely.

Perhaps the person following him was a private detective, watching the kissers. Probably not. What if the person was Law? But it was not Law's style. He always made his presence known. Perhaps it was another test put in place by The Owls of Athena. He was loathed to move from the stall in case he found himself in a street where nobody walked. Ryan sipped his coffee. Far too sweet. But it was hot. Very hot. He could throw it into the face of his assailant.

Nobody stood out from the crowd. Had he imagined it all? Paranoia? Perhaps weeks of stress were finally catching up. He jabbed his thumb and index fingers into his eyes and massaged gently. How many canisters had he placed around the city? He could not remember. Many hundreds he was sure. Not for the first time, Ryan suffered a sudden bout of guilt, and considered going to the authorities and coming clean. And then what? Someone else would be employed to do the dirty work. If he wanted to survive, this was the price.

A memory of childhood struck him. A quote from the Godforsaken church he was forced to attend for a period. He hated it. An antiquated, gothic building that seemed so out of place in the city, surrounded by the modern. It felt like being stuck in some unfamiliar past while there. Where his mother found solace in her faith, Ryan found frustration. It left him with more questions and a lingering anger toward those who had faith.

You will hear of wars and rumours of wars, but see to it that you are not alarmed. These things must happen, but the end is still to come.

He patted the shelf of the coffee stall and walked out into the rain, taking his unfinished coffee with him. He moved with brisk purpose, passed through the main streets of the city, and out to the quieter ones. The windows of the buildings he passed were empty. The streets darkened. He wanted to get back to his apartment. A closed door with a heavy bolt would keep him safe.

Ryan rounded a corner into another street.

"Ryan Bannister? I need you to kneel on the ground with your hands on your head. Do it now."

Ryan took a step back, squeezed his coffee cup a little too tight, and the hot liquid spilt over to his hand. "Shit," he complained, dropping the cup and shaking his hand. His one and only defensive weapon was gone.

The figure before him wore sweat pants and reached behind his back.

A blonde female, dressed in a similar manner, stepped closer to Ryan's left.

"Do as he says," she urged.

"I've done nothing wrong. I don't know you. You can't touch me. I'm not doing anything unless I see a badge."

"I won't ask a second time. We're Special Agents. Down on your knees and hands on your head. Slow."

"Let me see a badge, and then we'll talk."

Both agents drew weapons. Neither aimed directly at Ryan, but in a heartbeat they could have him dead.

"Last chance," the male agent said.

Flight won over fight. Ryan ran. He ran blindly. He turned and moved as fast as he could back the way he came. Two gunshots rang out. Ryan dived to the ground. He rolled into the verge, scampering behind a trashcan, and focused on every part of his body to work out where he had been hit. There was no pain. Is that what it was like? He'd heard adrenalin often kept pain at bay. But no ten metres behind him the male agent lay on the ground, arms wide and unmoving. A third figure stood over the female agent. She too lay on the ground, clutching her shoulder.

"Ryan, get over here, now."

Ryan peeped over the trashcan. "Who are you?"

"Law. Come over here, now." Law kicked a gun away from the female's reach. "Pick that up."

Ryan sprung upright and did as ordered. The weight of the handgun felt foreign and clumsy. He reached Law's side and for the first time saw the face that belonged to the phone voice. Law was nearing fifty, slim and wore a woollen hat.

"What do I do with it?" He held it gingerly between two palms, not wanting his fingers to discover the trigger.

"You never holstered a gun?"

"No."

Law stood over the wounded female. "How soon until your backup arrives?"

"Go to hell!"

"Soon enough we'll all be there." Law fired twice. A round into her head and one into her heart.

Ryan dropped the gun to the ground. "What are you doing?"

"Saving you." Law looked up to the surrounding buildings. Faces were at windows. He retrieved the handgun and shoved it at Ryan's stomach. "We need to go."

Ryan instinctively clutched the handgun close. Law grabbed his arm and pushed him aside with enough force that his feet scurried beneath him and he almost fell.

Law fired a round into the chest of the male agent.

"Stop shooting every one!"

"A cautionary shot. Dead men tell no tales. Keep up."

Law broke into a brisk pace. Ryan chased holding the barrel in a closed fist. They ran through streets, pounding puddles and knocking aside other street users. Behind them, sirens blared.

Law halted at a banged up Hyundai and pulled a set of keys from his pocket.

"Get in."

Ryan brushed aside fast food trash to find the seat. "Your diet could do with a bit of work," he said low enough for Law not to hear.

Law did not wait for Ryan to be seated. He started the car and drove. Fast.

"Whoa!" complained Ryan, the handgun falling to the floor.

"Buckle up."

Ryan grabbed the seatbelt and locked it in. "What's going on?"

"It's starting," replied Law, matter-of-factly. "We're leaving. Certain authorities became aware of some of our plans and took measures to intervene."

"I need to get to my apartment. There's things there I need."

Law laughed, his eyes never leaving the road ahead. "They're watching your apartment. There's no going back there now. Forget about what you had there. This city is about to die and you're being given a chance to escape."

Ryan leaned back into his seat. He clutched the handle of the door. Law drove like a racing car enthusiast.

"So it's really happening?"

Law didn't reply.

It was really happening. This was the beginning of the end. Ryan did not know how long it would take for Seattle to succumb but he guessed the sheer quantity of canisters would ensure the process was quick, but the agony would last much, much longer.

"What happens now? Whoa! Whoa!"

Law drove through a stop sign. Horns blasted.

"You're not a good passenger?"

"No," he whined.

"Time to change that. We're going to an old airfield outside the city. We're leaving the country. Further than that, I don't know. We'll change cars twice before we get there. We'll be pursued so keep that close." Law nodded to the weapon by Ryan's feet.

"I don't know how to use it."

"You point it and you pull the trigger."

Ryan's complicity in this whole thing had doomed hundreds of thousands of people to death. Yet the idea of pointing a gun and ending someone's life made his skin crawl. Hypocritical? Yes, he knew that. But that was how he felt, and yes, it made him to be a coward of sorts. But he'd be a coward that lived.

They drove on through the dying, dark city. The rain continued to fall as if tears, mourning the losses to come.

***

They changed cars twice, each vehicle an expensive executive car that looked pristine and showroom quality. An intense gun battle ensued with a police patrol. Ryan hunkered down into the foot well of the passenger seat, keeping his focus at his shoes as if somehow not looking would save him.

"Get up!" Law yelled.

"No!"

"Get up!"

"I can't!"

"What good are you?"

More shooting.

"You can take me home if I'm useless. I don't mind." He *was* useless. And in such a predicament, he preferred to be so.

More shooting, then silence.

"Can I get up now?"

"I don't know. Can you?"

"Did you kill the police?"

"What do you think?"

Law and Ryan arrived at the airfield. It was early morning. The term airfield was a generous expression. A temporary runway had been created inside a massive field, ploughed into compliance and developed for the sole purpose. It was miles from any population centre, deep into the Washington State countryside. Armed guards patrolled the perimeter. A Boeing 737 sat on the runway, two fuel tanks attended the aircraft.

The guards waved them to a halt and Law opened the window and received a handshake before being directed inside.

Law parked behind four fuel trucks. They stepped out of the car. Ryan's shoe splashed in the puddles on the ground. He sighed, and shook his foot free of the excess water. Law pulled several bags from the trunk and headed to the waiting aircraft.

Ryan matched his steps. "What happens now?"

Law checked his watch. "We're two hours from wheels up. Get settled on the plane. Don't talk to anyone, you understand me? Not a word. Get some sleep and when it's time you'll be told what to do."

"I've done everything you asked. I'm here and I don't know why. You owe me something. Tell me." Ryan tugged at Law's arm. "Law!"

Law dropped his bags, turned and grasped Ryan by the throat. A blade suddenly appeared at his cheek.

"Touch me again like that and I'll cut your face from your skull. Do not speak to me again." Law threw off Ryan, retrieved his bags and stomped off toward the aircraft.

Ryan stood alone in the field. The hum of the fuel trucks pumping and the low drone of the engines were the only sound. He closed his eyes. Ryan pretended he was heading somewhere pleasant, pretended he was back on a tarmac as he had been some years ago. He was heading to Mexico. He stood by the aircraft, shoulders high with genuine excitement at the adventure to come. It was bitterly cold but he was heading to blissfully warm Mexico.

The flight was comfortable. Bright coloured drinks were served by hostesses with lots of lipstick, and scarves tied at their neck. The heat when he landed was uncomfortable but a quick change into a pair of shorts and cotton shirt and he felt like a rich tourist. He wasted little time settling in, and headed out to the busy streets in search of some exciting nightlife. Scantily clad girls showed him attention, waving him over and blowing kisses, and suggesting they attend a party together in the bar they were there to promote. He could hear the sea rolling in not far away. People laughed. Music played. He was happy. He entered the bar. Cigar smoke hovered at eye level. Many moustached men fondled the breasts of women seated on their knees. The bartender looked unhappy. Perhaps he was tired. Perhaps he had pulled a double shift. A woman grabbed his hand and pulled him to a seat at the bar. Her finger played at the top button of her shirt.

"You are a very 'andsome boy. Would you like a drink? Beer? Tequila?"

"Tequila."

Ryan couldn't be sure what was in the tequila he was served, but he remembered little after his sixth drink, and woke up on the steps of his resort, shirt open, shorts on but no underwear beneath, and an empty wallet.

The engines revved, and Ryan was back in the field, back in a cold place, a place he took a personal hand in destroying, and knew nothing of their destination.

Ryan made his way to the 737. He climbed the stairs and passed a couple of armed guards who waved him on board. A woman in a tight fitting top and distracting combat pants welcomed him with a smile.

"Ryan Bannister?" she asked, her accent almost royally British.

"Yes. That's me."

"My name is Sonya Blake."

She was beautiful, even if she wore too much make-up. Blonde hair, tied back into a bun. Deep, blue eyes. Red, full lips. Slim but curvy in the right places. She was the type of woman who would never look twice at Ryan, but because of who he was she afforded him attention. But she could not be *just* a beautiful woman. The Owls of Athena hired people with specific skills. What might hers be?

"Mr. Bannister?"

Ryan was staring at her impolitely.

"No luggage?"

"I didn't have time to pack. I have no clothes other than what I'm in."

Sonya Blake touched his arm in a comforting way, and patted it twice. "All your needs will be taken care of once we reach our destination." She crossed his name off a manifest. "Allow me to show you to your seat. Please do not speak to your fellow passengers. This is the one rule of the flight."

He followed her down the aisle. It was not a huge plane. Maybe enough seats for around one-hundred-and-thirty or so. There was little room for comfort in the aircraft. Some curious and worried faces gazed his way. Some faces remained down, eyes reading files. Well-dressed men flicked through folders, pens in their hands, expensive glasses perched on their noses. They all had a look similar to Hector Crispin. An air of authority. An air of cash, and lots of it. Ryan imagined they were doctors, surgeons perhaps. Specialist surgeons. Perhaps neurosurgeons and paediatric surgeons and vascular surgeons. Some may have been gynaecologists or obstetricians. All sorts would be needed wherever they were going. The women and children sitting next to them were probably their family members. The women wore lots of jewellery. The children clung to backpacks and toys and books. One little girl gazed at Ryan, her eyes wide and worried. For a second he thought to smile and offer some comfort, but he looked away. He had no comfort to give. A woman in a thick coat nodded along to music coming from her headphones. She wasn't frightened. How was that possible? How could she not be terrified, or at minimum concerned? As if hearing his thoughts she looked up, seemed amused with his scrutiny, smiled, then returned to her music. Two large men in tracksuits sat side by side, their eyes closed, one already snoring. A long-haired teen, an earring in her nose, scowled at the closed tray in front of her.

The complement of passengers was an eclectic collection. He wondered if any had planted canisters as he had. He wondered if any that completed the same task as he were still alive. They were expendable, a potential liability with no particular skill.

He was ushered to a window seat toward the rear of the aircraft, and hit his head on the overhead lockers. He hoped no one noticed his awkwardness.

"You may alert me if you need anything. There will be some entertainment for the flight, or you may sleep. I'm sure it's been a long and difficult day. I'll bring you some water and something to eat. Sit back and relax. You're safe now. We'll be taking off within the next two hours."

His arms and legs ached from tension. He smelled bad. He had not showered in the last twenty-four hours. He looked like hell. Did it matter?

The gun that Law told him to grab remained in the car. It had slipped his mind to retrieve it. Maybe he should have been more focused. But he was surrounded by armed guards. They could do all the shooting.

Ryan closed his eyes. He did not open them when he felt the seat next to him become occupied. Ryan surrendered to sleep.

***

Jane stood in the kitchen making sandwiches for the family. The kids were watching Disney movies in the living room with their mom. The house felt strange without Eric. It was not as if she no longer felt safe, for Carter provided protection with his reassuring presence. Eric was simply gone and it hurt Jane, much like it hurt Jacqui, too. Neither spoke of it but both could recognise it in each other.

Carter paced from door to door, window to window, and repeated his watch over and again. He'd venture outside now and again, slowly walking the fence line and taking in what Jane assumed she could not hear or see. He made her uncomfortable as soldiers tended to do. Carter was an intense man, much like Eric, she supposed, but his voice was deep and humble and offered the feeling of a big protective rug. No harm would come to her, Jacqui or the kids, if he had any say in it.

Carter was standing by an ornate stone wishing well, a satellite phone to his ear. His fingers rubbed at his forehead. He clicked off the phone and walked into the kitchen.

"What's wrong?" Jane asked.

"Where's Jacqui?"

"Watching TV with the kids. Tell me."

"Eric's aircraft is missing. It disappeared from radar."

Jane dropped the knife she held. It clattered loudly to the floor.

Jacqui came in. "What happened?"

Jane picked up the knife and tried to appear calm. "It could be nothing. These things happen all the time."

"What? Tell me."

"Eric's aircraft disappeared off radar," Carter explained. "They can't raise communication with it or him."

Jacqui couldn't have stood straighter. "And what does that mean?"

"It's not confirmed as a crash. Machinery might have malfunctioned and they were forced to land."

Jacqui grabbed Jane's hands and stilled them. The two women looked to each for support.

"What do you think happened, Carter?" asked Jacqui. "Don't bullshit us."

"I'd expect that if they had landed somewhere they'd be trying to raise the alarm. No communication isn't good, but if anyone can—"

"I know my husband, thank you, Carter. I know what he's capable of. Jane, if the sandwiches are ready, my children are hungry."

"He'll be alright," said Jane.

"Yes, he will," Jacqui said softly. "If you will excuse me, I need a moment to myself."

***

Brutus prowled the corridors of the first floor. He dared not penetrate too far into the interior and risk being spotted. The building was not operational. Some rooms required doors. Exposed wires dangled from security cameras. Furniture was still boxed and piled in corners. And the near constant stream of deliveries suggested final completion was being rushed.

Brutus tapped the barrel of his Glock on the door of a closed room. Nothing. No questioning voice. He nudged the door open. Inside was spacious, dominated by a long, wooden table. Fifteen chairs were tucked beneath, and still wrapped in protective plastic. An enormous TV was mounted on the wall. Off to the right, a sink and some kitchen units with an integrated hot tap. It would not have looked out of place in a conference centre. As much as he wanted to map out each room, he knew time was short, and his priority was to identify how susceptible the building was to his plans. So far, very, but only if he moved quickly.

Brutus made his way back to the maintenance stairwell then retreated back to ground level. He halted at the doorway, chancing a glance out into the courtyard. They were still unloading. Thirty minutes had passed since he killed the driver.

Brutus flicked up his collar and made a beeline for the lorry. Nobody paid him much heed. He hopped up into the cabin and closed the door, cranking the window a little, enough to hear if anyone approached.

The team moved empty pallets and roll cages into the trailer. One of the team slapped the side of the cabin and whistled. "You're good to go. Get the wagon turned around and out of here."

Brutus waved and started the engine. He turned the wagon in the yard and pulled up slowly to the gate. The guards waved him through after the briefest of inspections.

He needed more men, only for two days, and they would take the building and be protected from the pandemic to come.

CHAPTER 5

AND YOU WILL HEAR RUMOURS

Perhaps it was Gemma's imagination or perhaps reality, but gunshots came more often. Jacob told her two of the administration staff attempted to escape after one was bitten by an infected. They made it less than five-hundred metres from the facility before being brought back in body bags. She wanted to scream to the world about what was happening there. Someone had to listen. But if help was coming it would have arrived by now.

Jacob pestered her hourly. She used promises and threats to keep his panic under some level of control.

"Tomorrow," she often told him. "We'll be out of the hospital tomorrow."

But she could no longer believe that might be true. Food supplies dwindled. Fresh foods were no longer available. Cereal bars in boxes. Tinned biscuits. Dried fruits in bags, and tinned peaches in jelly, and meals ready for nuking in the microwave. Nothing appealing.

Even the patrolling soldiers complained. "You'd think they'd keep we peace-keeping workers fed with decent stuff."

The soldiers were not stone-cold killers, she reasoned. They had families. Loved ones. People they left behind. And bodies that required hardy foods to function. Perhaps they would slacken in their resolve. Hungry people struggled to focus, didn't they? Hungry people would be hesitant to obey orders, no?

"Gemma." Her own personal stalker appeared. "I was thinking. Maybe we should stick together until they come. You know, so nothing can go wrong." He looked over his shoulder, then whispered, "There was more shooting this morning. This place is falling apart."

"Jacob," said Gemma patting his arm, "we can't do that. If the soldiers notice we're spending too much time together they'll ask some pretty serious questions. We need to be smart about this. When they come, we'll both get out of here. I promise. But we need to keep ourselves safe until then."

Jacob nodded emphatically. "You're right. Christ, it's just all the shooting and people disappearing and not coming back. We wait much longer, and it'll be you or me that's gone and never coming back."

"That's why we're getting out of here, Jacob. Trust me."

He pinched the bridge of his nose. "I do, Gemma."

"That building in Glasgow, the one you worked on. It's easy to find, yes?"

"It's not like anything else in the city. But you shouldn't think of going there. It's dangerous. Look what happened to me. Where will you go once you're out of here?"

Gemma sighed. "I'm going home to my parents. I'm going to make sure they're safe."

"Then what?"

Gemma's plan consisted of getting out of the hospital and blackmailing Black Aquila with the information to ensure her parents were safe. Beyond that, she had no plans. Watch the world fall apart from somewhere safe?

"I'm not sure, Jacob. What about you?"

Jacob steered Gemma away from the window, as if someone outside would be able to hear. "I'm going to get as far away from people as I can. When I was younger my friends and I would go camping. There was a spot, fresh water running nearby. Miles from anywhere. Animals to hunt. Sheltered from the elements. I'll stay there until everything settles down."

"That's a good plan, Jacob. It's good you're thinking about what comes next."

"We'll get through this together. You and I. Our fates are locked, Gemma. I'm sorry about how I was when we first met. I know I've said sorry before but I was scared and I didn't know how to get out. I'll leave you now. Come get me if you hear anything. I'll be in my usual place."

A thought struck her as she watched him go. So much of the hospital was not in use. The decline of patients perhaps was testament to the virility of the Carrion Virus. How long until the guards fell victim? Gemma did not intend to find out.

Gemma left the confinement of the uppermost levels and headed down to one of the communal areas still in operation. Exhausted staff filled the room, all were silent. Some lay across chairs with their eyes closed. Some read crumpled paperbacks. A TV broadcasted endless stories of the crisis. The reporting was extremely understated. The mainstream media for all intents and purposes was now a tool to control the fear of the panicked population.

Gemma pulled up a chair next to three women and a male. They looked like administration staff. The male rested his head on the table. Asleep?

"Tough day?" she asked the group.

The woman closest to her spoke without drawing her eyes away from the TV. "That's all there is around here now."

"I can see that," said Gemma. "How long have you been here?"

The woman looked at Gemma with a hopeless frustration. "You ask a lot of questions and that's not a wise thing to do here."

"Last I checked, this was Britain and it was alright to do that."

The male raised his head. "Does this look like the kind of Britain you recognise? Ask yourself that."

Gemma caught a glimpse of his badge. He was a staff nurse. William Wozniack.

"Hush, William," said the woman closest to Gemma. "You can't say that."

"I'm sorry, Morag, but it's about time we started saying things. Complaining. We're being treated like prisoners here. Told it's for our own protection and that we're serving the nation by our commitment. I don't see that anymore. We're allowing this to go on. This isn't medicine. This isn't anything we should be part of."

"Please, William. They'll hear."

"I agree with you, William," said Gemma. "What's going on here isn't right. What I've seen and what I've been told isn't helping people. It's hurting them. We can't just sit back. When was the last time you were home, or were allowed to call your family?"

Morag paused, her mouth open with a half formed word. She closed her mouth and wiped her eyes with a crumpled napkin. "Three weeks. It's been three weeks."

"I could go around the table here and ask you all the same and I'd bet all the tea in China that you'd say the same. This isn't right."

"Oh God." Morag looked past Gemma.

Gemma turned. An armed soldier made his way through the communal area toward their table.

"What's going on here?" asked the soldier. "You know the rules about this kind of thing."

"What?" said Gemma. "Sitting at a table and saying hello?"

"You know what I mean."

"We were discussing the situation here," said Gemma. "There's nothing wrong with that, is there?"

"There's something wrong with causing trouble. Maybe you should consider that before you go opening your mouth, love?"

Love? Gemma did not like being addressed in that fashion, nor did she like his smug look, nor the way he towered over her expecting her to crumble with terror.

"What is the military so afraid of? We nobodies having a chat? We're being treated like prisoners and slaves here. Are we not even allowed to discuss the truth, *love?*"

Morag turned a ghostly shade of white and held her napkin to her mouth. William watched with a horrified fascination, poised to take cover at a moment's notice.

"What's your name?" asked the soldier.

"Piss off," said Gemma.

"Come with me." The soldier reached down and grabbed Gemma by the arm.

"Hey!"

He hauled her easily out of the seat and to her feet.

William was on his feet in an instant. "Leave her alone. She hasn't done anything wrong."

The soldier pointed to William. "Sit down and shut up. I'm in charge here."

"No," William argued defiantly. "Let her go this minute!"

Others stood and joined in the chorus. More and more joined in and their demands grew to shouts.

The soldier threw Gemma back into the seat. She hit her chest against the table edge. Her breath burst from her lungs and she grunted with the pain. The soldier brought his weapon up, and everyone fell to the floor or scattered, but not William.

"What will you do, soldier? Shoot us all? And for what? Asking questions? They're questions that need to be asked. When was the last time you were allowed to speak to your family? Do you have a wife? Girlfriend? Out there?" William pointed to the window. "The country is changing every day and we're stuck here in a bubble where we don't know what's happening to our families. We're here because we want to help, but the asking price is too high. We can't not know."

The soldier's weapon slipped an inch.

"Nobody here would deny helping those in need but we're not machines," said Gemma. "We all give something but we need something back, too."

"We've let it go on for too long," added William. "We're not asking for the world, just our basic rights."

Morag wept in the corner. "Please, just let us speak to our families. I don't know if they're okay. Please."

The soldier backed away. He glared at Gemma, then each person he passed.

"This isn't something that will go away," shouted William. "You need to address this. Get your superiors in here to talk otherwise you'll find us unwilling to work."

Shouts of agreement came.

"Today there's a handful of us. Tomorrow we'll bring this facility to a standstill."

Gemma crossed to William. She hugged him gingerly. "Thank you for speaking up."

"Something has to be done," he said evenly.

"We can't let it end here. We need to spread tell all staff in this facility. We're only a handful. They can't ignore all of us. We need to make something happen."

The seeds were planted. This mini revolt increased her opportunities to leave. It was an entirely self-serving endeavour even if others would benefit from it. Gemma rubbed her chest. It would probably be a bruise tomorrow.

***

Ice cold water dripped into Eric's face. The sensation brought him back from a dark place, back into the world. Nothing made sense. For the longest time he could not rationalise his situation. He lay on his back, crumpled metal and the twisted and broken body of the Chinook nearby. It was snow dripping from the tree branches overhead that encouraged his return to consciousness. He shivered uncontrollably. It was daylight. He had no idea how long he had been out. When they crashed it was night-time. He could have lain out in the elements for five hours at least. It was a miracle he had not succumbed to the freezing temperatures.

Eric wiped the wet from his forehead, but recoiled in pain. He touched a significant gash on his forehead. He tried to sit up but vomited.

Got to move. So cold.

Eric pushed himself to his feet, holding himself against the wall section of the aircraft. His pack and weapon remained strapped to him. Above, the forest canopy was torn where the aircraft came down. Metres away fires smouldered.

"Hello?" shouted Eric. "Anyone hear me?"

Only his echo responded. The forest was winter quiet and still.

Eric hobbled. His legs were close to numb. He moved around the wreckage to the cockpit, stomping to return feeling to his legs, but with every thud, pain shuddered upwards. The front of the aircraft had taken most of the impact. The compartment was crushed into a barely recognisable puzzle. Blood stains and a protruding arm was all the evidence Eric needed to decipher the fate of the pilots.

He removed his pack, and the satellite phone he wore fell in pieces to the ground. He rummaged through the pack and pulled out a small field dressing kit. Nothing to clean the wound, but he found adhesive dressing. He pulled it free from the protective sheath and sucked in air as he applied pressure to his forehead.

He clasped a hand to his chest. Perhaps a broken rib, perhaps two. It was too cold to undress and inspect. He had to move or die. He reasoned help would have arrived if a distress call was sent. Or perhaps there was no one to receive it. Eric scavenged around the crash site but found little in the way of useful items. Much was lost on impact.

He'd have to search the area, find a trail, a track, a way to safety. He started in the direction where the trees began to thin. The ground was uneven, tripping him at every opportunity. *Lift your feet, Eric!* His legs didn't want to obey, and dragged too often, but the stumbles lessened and he made some distance.

The edge of the forest came suddenly. The trees fell behind and he was moving through untamed land. Beyond was a tapestry of farmland, old stone walls marking the boundaries between each field. No roads that he could make out, and no visible populated centres. The fields were neatly uniform. In the summer they would possibly support crops of some kind. There must be a farm nearby. Even a small village. He wished for binoculars. Or for an accurate map position.

Eric started over the first stone wall. The stones slipped and moved as he went. He landed hard on the ground. His left foot broke through ice hidden under the snow.

"Shit! Shit!" The water was freezing. He ripped his foot free, and the pain of the cold disappeared as numbness took over.

He needed shelter and heat. Eric got back to his feet, and limped, crossing two more walls and crested a hill. He doubled over and dry retched, then kept moving. Down into the small valley behind the hill, he could make out a farmstead, a cluster of buildings with smoke rising from a chimney. A road stretched into the distance. No traffic, probably just an access road to the farm. It was shelter. The farm would have a phone. He could contact Jacqui, let her know he was alive.

He wiped at his eyes, slapped at his cheeks, keen to dispel the threatening dizziness. *Got to keep going.* He made his way down the hill, slipping to his knees more than once. *Get up!* His whole body shook. His head burned.

"Getttt upppp!" he ordered, his teeth chattering. His limbs would not comply. His body folded, and suddenly he was face down in the snow. *Got to keep going.* A wall of sleep fell atop him. No matter how hard he fought against it, he could not resist. *Jacqui!*

***

News of Gemma's stand against the soldier spread like wildfire. Medical and support staff gathered in the communal area, turning it into an unofficial picket line. Nothing too intimidating. It was just a collection of frightened and broken staff making a stand against what they felt was an almost tyrannical dictatorship. Gemma would have felt a miniscule of pride if she were not entirely motivated by her own interests.

Two soldiers stood by the doors. Neither were threatening in manner, and were more like interested onlookers. The room smelt unpleasant. Double shifts and little time for showers made body odours triple.

William said to a doctor, "They're not monsters those soldiers. They're people like you and I following orders. Perhaps illegal orders. But there won't be violence as a result of this."

The doctor played with his stethoscope. "I keep thinking of the infected patients they remove. Who gives an order like that?"

"Gemma," William said, "how do you think this will go down? I'm a little worried despite what I say to the others."

"What's been your experience of the soldiers?"

"At the start, we welcomed them. They were here to protect us and maintain our ability to work. Then later, they became our jailers. The original reason for them being here feels forgotten. We're no longer on the same page. They're here to keep us in check, and keep the infected from getting out. Or in."

"William, they can't do anything to us. If they don't play it safe, this facility becomes useless. You and the other staff are the blood of this place, and it needs you to keep pumping."

"I don't like that everyone looks to me for some kind of guidance. There's doctors here. Men and women smarter and more able to lead."

"But it was you that took a stand. That counts for a lot."

"*We* took a stand, Gemma."

"Yes. We did. And it was the right thing to do."

"I hope you're right."

"Ask yourself this. As a medical professional, could you endure much more of this? The situation?"

William considered it for a moment. "No," he said finally. "No, I don't think many of us could have."

"Then it's the right thing to do."

William smiled, nodding his thanks. He turned to the closest group and inserted himself into their conversation.

A commotion at the doorway drew the attention of the crowd. Gemma stretched up on her tiptoes. More soldiers filed into the room. All armed but they held their weapons down. A man in a suit, balding and almost penguin-like in his hurried, clumsy walk appeared between the soldiers.

"Ladies and gentlemen," he shouted, holding his hands in the air. "Ladies and gentlemen, if I can have your attention. My name is Myles Swanson. I am the government appointed agent for this facility. Due to several factors, not least being this mutiny you have staged, the military support for this facility is being withdrawn and redeployed immediately." He scowled, his nose lifting in indignation, as if each one of them played a part in offending him personally. "Please wait here until we have evacuated. Thank you for your time."

"They're going?"

"What about us?"

"What will happen to us?"

"Who will protect us?"

"You can't do this!"

"What if the infected break loose?"

Whilst everyone was panicking, Gemma wanted to cheer. Her avenue to escape was only moments away. She waited for as long as she dared, then skirted the outside of the group, and on to the door. The corridor was empty.

"They told us to wait here," complained one of the staff.

"I'm not going anywhere," she said quietly.

She listened intently. No gunshots or screams. The hospital was quiet like the grave.

"I'll check what's going on. Wait here." She pushed through the doors, walked quickly past the wards and past patients.

Jacob waved from his doorway. "They're gone."

"Are you sure?"

"They told us to stay in our beds until the medical staff returned."

"We're going."

"Now?"

"Grab your stuff."

Jacob pulled on a thick winter coat, grabbed his backpack and followed Gemma. She grabbed a coat and her backpack from a hidden cupboard in the corridor. Jacob was slow.

"Come on," she called.

"I'm trying."

The carpark was empty of military presence. The roadblock had been dismantled and the road lay open. Civilian cars filled the northern end. Snow had compacted on windscreens, and some wheels looked buried in white.

"Will they start?" Jacob complained.

"Of course they will. Check the reception desks for car keys."

Jacob returned inside and Gemma ran to the northern end and tried door handles. All were locked. She bound through a layer of snow to get to more cars just around the corner. All locked, too.

"Gemma, where are you?"

"Here!"

"I've got a key!"

"Start clicking the button. See which car it opens."

The telling *beep* of a car being unlocked sent Gemma back to the northern carpark. Jacob had clicked open a Citroën hatchback.

"Start her up," she ordered.

Jacob slipped into the driver's seat. The engine burst into life without a hint of effort. He wound down the window.

"Would you look at that? Started first time. Someone must have been turning it over regularly."

Gemma reached the car and swiped at the snow on the window. "Shit. It's not budging. Look for something in the car."

"Like what?"

"Something to shift this shit."

Jacob dived into the back seat and came back up with a plastic scraper. "This do?"

"Here!"

He tossed it across the bonnet. Gemma started chipping away. Progress was slow.

Jacob called out, "There's almost a full tank."

"Come out and take over, Jacob."

"Righteo." He did as he was asked and went to work on the ice.

Gemma inspected the rear tyres. Snow banked around them. Forward motion was going to be difficult. One of them would need to push, and she knew it would be her. She kicked at the snow, chipping away at the weeks of accumulation.

William stood at the doorway to the hospital. "Gemma?"

"We need to go. Now!"

"I haven't budged much," Jacob said with panic. "It's not enough to drive."

"It'll have to do. Get in, I'll push."

Jacob pushed the accelerator and the wheels spun and spat out snow and slush. Much of it hit Gemma, but she rocked the car with all the strength she could muster.

"Gemma!" William descended the steps.

The car lurched forward, but not enough. She replanted her feet and pushed and pushed. Jacob floored the accelerator, throwing up a fountain of white, and the car escaped its snow tomb.

Gemma pulled off her backpack and jumped into the passenger seat. "Drive!"

"What about him?"

William was only metres away.

"Just drive."

"Where?"

"Are you really such an idiot? Just drive, Jacob."

"Okay, okay."

He put the car in gear and drove.

***

Jane sat at the dinner table eating yet another muesli bar. She would have loved a bowl of fresh strawberries and pears for dessert, and a huge helping of chocolate ice-cream, but the shops didn't offer those anymore. Oats rolled into a bar with honey and preservatives and wrapped in foil paper were her treats now.

Carter never seemed to be still in one place for long. He circumnavigated the rooms yet again as she chewed and longed for something fresher. His shirt could not hide the weapon tucked into his belt. Carter peeked through the split in the curtains. He touched a finger to his ear, pressing the small headphone bud. She knew he monitored several channels and public radio. But he never shared what he heard.

"Get you some coffee, Carter?" Jane pointed to the kettle.

Carter shook his head, turned back from the window and put his hand over his ear.

"It's hot."

He waved her to silence, and pulled out a small notepad from his pocket. He motioned for something to write with. Jane rolled a pen toward him.

"Suppose a muesli bar wouldn't interest you either?" she said quietly.

He scribbled, his face a mask of neutrality, then dropped the pen, pulled the earphone free and rubbed his temples.

"What is it? Something's wrong?"

"It's starting," he said evenly. He did not look up. He didn't seem alarmed. He just appeared resigned. "There's outbreaks reported at the major cities. The car's packed?"

"Yes. We did what you said." They had prepared for emergencies. Essentials were packed into the car. The fuel tank was full. Carter had even practised a speedy exit five times, the kids finding it great fun to get faster with each try.

"Good. Go get Jacqui without worrying the kids. Can you do that?"

Jane stood from the table. "How close is the outbreak? How near are they to us?"

"We need to move quickly."

"Carter?"

"Very close. This isn't common knowledge so we can beat the panic that is certain to come."

"Can we get help?"

"We are the help. Now please get Jacqui."

Jane ran to the dark living room. The TV gave off a little light. "Jacqui, Carter is wondering if he could have a word with you in the kitchen."

Jacqui looked to her with alarm, but didn't say a word, just casually left the couch. "I'll be back in a minute, kids."

The kids were too focused on the TV to care.

"What is it?" she whispered when away from the kids.

"It's happening. We need to move."

"Now?"

"Yes."

Carter called out, "Turn the lights off, now."

Jacqui and Jane obeyed immediately and plunged the house into darkness.

"Mom!"

"Grab the kids," ordered Carter. "They *must* be silent."

Jacqui was gone before Carter could finish his sentence. Jane was by Carter's side in the kitchen. He was pulling the assault rifle down from the top cupboard, the rifle Williamson provided.

"What's going on, Carter?"

There was a click as Carter loaded the rifle.

"They're here." He screwed a long silencer to the end of the weapon and slung the bag of ammunition over his shoulder.

Jane rushed to the window. Down the road, in the street, people milled about outside a house. From this distance, it seemed they were dancing a fast and violent jig. But she knew better. The infected, once seen, were impossible to forget. They had time, there was a lot of houses between there and here. But Jane felt a storm of fear ready to rip her in two.

"You've seen this all before, Jane. You know what to do. Jane?"

"Yes. Yes, I know." She breathed in deeply, one long breath and held it for four seconds, then followed Carter into the living room.

"Quietly now, everyone. Kids, just like we practised, we're going to leave the house."

"No talking, kids, remember?" said Jane.

The kids nodded their understanding.

"Once we walk through the front door, you look to me for direction. You do what I say. You watch for my hand signals." Carter looked between Jacqui and Jane. "We're going to be okay. I promise you that. We head to the safe house. You remember the directions I gave you? If something happens to me, you know where to go, right?"

The women nodded. Jacqui helped Luke and Katie into their coats.

"I'll lead, go out and open each door. Jacqui, you take Luke. Jane, take Katie. Get them strapped in."

"We know," said Jane. "That's how we practised."

Carter almost smiled. He unlocked the heavy door, stepped out into the night, weapon ready. He moved steadily, scanning with the rifle. He reached the car and pulled the keys from his pocket, unlocked the vehicle and opened each door in turn. The internal lights did not flicker on. Carter had removed the globes earlier, and at the same time he had covered the head and tail lights with duct tape.

Carter scanned the perimeter then signalled the group to leave the house. Jacqui led with Luke in her arms. Jane followed behind, holding Katie's hand. With each step, Jacqui turned making sure Katie was safe.

Jane's hands shook, making snapping the seatbelt to lock difficult. Jacqui leaned into the car, took over and locked the belt in place. Jacqui squeezed her way into the middle seat in the back of the car, between the two kids. Jane jumped into the front seat.

The infected trampled the garden beds of a house five doors down. That front door was ajar, so too, the door to the house across the road.

Jane knew what that meant. Those neighbours were doomed. They needed to be going.

Despite all the practicing, Katie grew anxious. She whimpered. Jacqui placed her hand over her mouth, and whispered soft words into her daughter's ear. Jane silently pleaded for Carter to get into the car and drive. But Carter's rifle was up. The rabble turned their way. Some sniffed at the air. Dark shapes appeared from some of the houses, their attention pointed at the car.

Carter swore. He pulled the keys from his pocket and threw them to Jane.

"Drive," he ordered.

Carter fired and two heads burst open. Jane pushed herself from the passenger seat, scrambled over the gear shift and into the driver's seat. She started the engine, and put it into gear. Luke's cries joined Katie's.

"Carter!" shouted Jacqui.

Jane released the handbrake. The car rolled forward.

Carter blasted the infected closing in on the driveway. They fell, but one crawled further on its belly. It was fast, its jaws snapping. Carter bolted to the car and dived in. Jane stepped on the accelerator. The car bounced over the crawling infected. Out on the roadway she hit three bodies. They bounced off the bonnet. Luke and Katie screamed. Jane swerved and swerved again.

"Keep the tyres on the road," ordered Carter.

"I'm trying!"

Two jumped onto the bonnet of the car, their faces at the windscreen.

"Mum! Mum!"

"Shhh, honey. We'll be alright!"

"Go! Go! Go!" Carter pulled his Glock free.

"Go where?" said Jane. "I can't see!"

"Left! Go left! Now!"

Jane tugged the wheel hard. The bodies slid across the bonnet and onto the ground.

"Floor it!"

"Where are they all coming from?" shrieked Jacqui.

The engine roared. The kids whimpered. They were away, away from the danger.

"Check your mirrors," ordered Carter.

Empty roads. "Nothing," said Jane.

"Mummy, what where they?" asked Katie.

"They were your neighbours," Carter explained with no emotion.

***

Eric awoke to confusion. He was no longer cold, no longer subjected to the elements, no longer believing he was about to die. He was in a room, the wallpapered walls busy with swirling patterns. Musty curtains were half-pulled across the only window. Photos of people he did not know hung on the walls alongside paintings of landscapes and cities he could not place. A log fire pumped out an intense heat, a block of wood sparking and spitting. His head rested on bumpy pillows on a fold-down sofa. A thick eiderdown covered him from chest to feet. Eric ached all over, and stiffness made everything feel locked.

A black and white Collie lay on a padded bed on the floor. It looked at Eric with a lazy interest, one ear moving searching for sound.

He beckoned the dog with his hand. The Collie stretched and yawned before jumping up onto the bed. The motion kicked off a stabbing pain in Eric's chest. He petted the dog. *SKYE* was engraved on a silver medallion attached to its collar.

"Hello, girl." His throat was raw, his voice crackling like the fire.

Skye licked Eric's face.

"Skye, get down!" An older women, her hair tied back into a tight bun, pointed to the dog's bed. Skye obeyed and nestled back on her bed.

"It's good to see you awake finally. We've been calling you John. Doesn't seem to fit now you're awake."

"Eric," he coughed. "Eric Mann."

"Well, Eric Mann, I'm Hazel Ingram."

"Let's get some water into you, shall we?" She held a glass to his lips. "Slow now. Don't want you choking. You've not had much since you've been here."

He chugged at the water, not stopping to wince at the sting in his throat.

"Slow now. You've been with us for, oh, I think this is the fourth day now. You were lucky my husband Allan was out walking the dog in the snow. You lying there out cold. If you'd been there for much longer then ... well, I suppose that doesn't matter now, does it?"

"Anyone know I'm here?"

"We rang the authorities. But they never came." Hazel shook her head. "Things have gotten strange of late."

"Strange?"

She laughed. "Inquisitive aren't we? Well, yesterday the television went down. It's as if the signal isn't there. Then the power started to go off and on. Now we're using paraffin lamps and have to heat our own water. We've not seen a soul for days now, except you."

"What about the radio?" He moved and winced at the pain.

"Now you lay still there. Plenty of time to mend. Allan hasn't put the radio on for a few days. He says things are bad enough."

"I need to know what's happening."

"So the soldier's awake?" A tall man appeared at the doorway, a well-maintained shotgun at his side. He stood with a firm confidence that left Eric certain he was entirely capable of using the firearm, and using it well.

"Oh for Godsakes, Allan. Put that thing away." Hazel left the bedside and pushed the barrel of Allan's firearm toward the ground.

Allan walked to the corner of the room and sank down into a creaky, old chair. He rested the shotgun between his legs, reached down and scratched Skye behind the ear.

"Allan, this is Eric. And you're to remember he's our guest. He was asking for our radio."

"He can have the radio after he's answered some questions. What were you doing out in the snow all banged up? You're a soldier?"

"I'm not a soldier. I work for Black Aquila, a security company. I was in a crash."

"Why were you flying overhead?"

"Heading to help a friend. She's in a difficult position."

"Is all this connected to the troubles up in Aberdeen?"

"Yes. I won't impose any longer. I need to get back." He moved and cringed.

"Oh no, young man. Your legs won't carry you far. You need to rest up."

Allan stood from the chair. "Give him the radio. I'm going to take Skye out for a walk."

"Another one? You'll have her run to skin and bones before you're done."

"You know she likes the exercise. Come on, girl."

Skye leapt up, her tail wagging wildly.

"Sit, girl," he ordered, and the obedient dog did as instructed, her eyes keen for the next instruction. Allan studied Eric, a warning in his glare. "Come," he said to the dog, and they were both gone.

"Well let me get that radio for you, Eric. Forgive Allan if he comes across as overbearing. These are unusual days, and he's a little uptight."

Hazel headed off. A door banged loudly and footsteps could be heard on a veranda outside. The dog barked; they were happy sounds. The swirling patterns on the wallpaper were actually floral images. A log in the fire rolled. Skye's barks were further off.

Hazel returned. "Give it a good crank. It's quite old. I'll leave you to it. If you need anything else you can just shout."

"Are your phones working?"

"They were. Not anymore."

Eric wound up the old radio and flicked the switch. The radio burst into life, hissing static. He extended the aerial and twisted the dial. Faint voices broke through the distortion but not enough to understand. He picked up the odd word here and there, and played with the dial again.

"Outbreaks ... secure yourself ... following routes are to be avoided ... London, Birmingham, Manchester, Newcastle, Nottingham ... virus has been reported ... do not approach ... "

It happened. Williamson was right.

CHAPTER 6

ARISE, A KING.

And there stood his prize waiting to be claimed. Brutus had run his plan through his head so many times his skull thumped. It was a large building with a lot of walls to patrol. It would hold back a tide of infected. It was perfect.

Brutus could have skulked off to some remote, tropical island, a place where the virus would likely never reach, away from a dying city. But where would be the fun in that? Brutus liked violence. He could not say why, nor did he really care. Brutus did what Brutus wanted.

Security was minimal; to avoid attention he assumed. An attack now would be preferable. His team was due to arrive in two hours, their families in tow.

More aircraft buzzed overhead. Military mostly, with a splattering of civilian. The signs were pointing toward something happening imminently, and Brutus's guess was that guests of The Owls of Athena would arrive within the next seventy-two hours. And that pointed to the engineered outbreak coming, and soon.

Brutus walked back to his van, through puddles filled over and again by the incessant Glasgow rain. He reached in, pulled out his tac vest and strapped it on.

***

Everything felt different since landing in the UK. Ryan Bannister allowed himself to be ushered along, a spectator to his own existence. He placed utter trust in The Owls of Athena. There was no alternative really. Without them, he would likely be one of the infected by now. Or dead. But what he did in Seattle, his home city, to think about it now made bile rise. Telling himself that he had no choice, true or not, did not help. The consequence of survival was to be haunted by his actions.

When the plane landed they were met by heavy security, ushered onto two buses and again instructed not to speak to other passengers. Three escort vehicles guided the buses north. Ryan fell asleep three times, and excused himself just as many times to use the toilet at the back of the bus. He was nervous. He was fidgeting. His cell was out of charge and there was little to do. Someone snored loudly. The woman next to him read a battered paperback while music blared from her headphones. Her head swayed to the music now and again. Through the little music Ryan could hear, it was classical stuff, something very melancholic. The cover of her book suggested the novel was about a Japanese woman during wartime. The two didn't match. Beethoven and a geisha? And how could the woman listen to music *and* read a book? She was possibly a multi-skilled woman. Of course she was skilled. Everyone on the bus had some use, didn't they? He wanted to ask about her particular use. Curiosity was ready to burst from his busy fingers. But he knew the rules, knew to remain silent. He had witnessed what happened to people who didn't obey.

They moved through the streets of a city at night. London. He knew one of the sanctuaries to be located there. More than once the bus rocked violently as it rolled up onto the sidewalk to avoid congestion, before returning to the road. The cars they passed were filled with families, each vehicle stuffed with belongings, bag upon bag filling parcel shelves. Children slept between piles of clothes. A dog lay across the lap of a sleeping woman, one hand resting upon its back. These forlorn people were refugees.

But where did Ryan Bannister fit into all this? That remained to be seen.

The convoy ground to a halt. He could see the building in front. He recognised the design as a scaled down version of the one in Japan. Tall walls surrounded a monolithic building lit up against the oppressive night. Armed men moved at the gate ahead, waving the convoy into the courtyard. They slowly pulled in, the bus bouncing on a speed bump which ran the length of the gate. Floodlights within the courtyard broke the darkness. Ryan shielded his eyes until they adapted. They parked in a designated zone, following the instructions of a man in a reflective vest waving his hands about.

The coach door opened and one of the armed guards leapt up the steps.

"May I have your attention? You have reached your journey's end. Please exit the bus in an organised fashion and wait outside. Your names will be called. You will be processed then taken to rooms for rest. Food and drinks will be provided. This way, please."

Ryan stood. The ceaseless hours of inactivity were not kind to his legs. He squeezed his toes asking circulation to return. None of the passengers moved quickly. Seemed they all suffered the same pains. He looked down to their footwear as if he might see toes scrunching. Ryan was the first to exit the bus. The cold air at first was refreshing. He breathed deeply, then coughed, then wrapped his arms around himself and waited for the other travellers to alight.

The gate behind them moved, the small motor humming as the barrier wheeled back into place. Heavy mesh topped with razor wire spanned the height of the entrance. Up on the high perimeter walls men walked in patrol, none of them obviously armed. Smart. It made sense to conceal the building's true purpose. Ryan did not see them as they approached, he was too focused on the building itself.

In the shadow of the building two women sat behind a portable table, sheltered by an open-sided canopy. Artificial light from laptops illuminated their faces. They smiled in welcome and began calling names. The new arrivals waited in silence, and when called spent no more than two minutes being processed. There did not seem to be an order, not alphabetical certainly. Not of age. Not of height. The cold bit at Ryan to the point he almost made a protest at the length of time they waited.

"Ryan Bannister?"

"Here." He stepped forward, arms wrapped around himself.

The woman sitting before him was pretty, late forties, and hair hidden by a woollen hat. Her lips defined her, artificially plump and red as blood. She watched him with a predator's interest, her dark eyes studying every part of him.

"Welcome to Sanctuary."

Sanctuary? Not very creative.

"Your journey is at an end. All we're doing at this point is registering you and giving you your keycard. It will allow you free passage around the areas of the building you're entitled to."

"I was hoping to speak with Hector Crispin tonight."

"That will not be possible. He has also just arrived from an arduous journey. Perhaps tomorrow. If he wants it to happen I am sure you will be summoned."

"I don't think you understand. Actually, I never caught your name?"

"Mr. Bannister, here we all have roles to fulfil. I'm doing mine. Let me sign you in. Get some rest and all your questions will be answered in due course. Here is your ID card. It also serves as your key, and as you can see it sits on the lanyard. It's important to wear it at all times."

Ryan placed the lanyard around his neck.

"Room thirteen. Fourth floor. Refreshments are available there."

"Hector Crispin *will* summon me."

"If you say so, Mr. Bannister. Enjoy your stay."

The lobby was large and vaulted. A guard stood at a very long, unmanned reception desk. He pointed to the stairs at the far end of the room. Ryan obeyed the silent direction. The lift access point was closed off. Four flights of stairs! His legs seemed to protest, and he looked at everyone else's legs expecting to see the same. But they all moved. So he moved, too.

The first floor mezzanine overlooked the entrance. A man with slicked back, dark hair stood with hands resting on the barrier, and watched as the new arrivals filtered in. Some of the travellers left the stairs and headed to their rooms. The same happened at the second and third floors. Ryan was suitably out of breath, and a little self-conscious about his lack of fitness when he arrived at the fourth floor. He had walked city streets for miles and miles, yet found four sets of stairs a challenge? *Must be the flight followed by the long bus ride. Too much of nothing.*

He walked up the corridor, studying each door. They all had the names of the occupants on a small sign to the side of the door. He reached room thirteen. To the left of the door, his name adorned a label above a doorbell, just like all the others. Below it, a scanner. Ryan touched his keycard to the scanner and the door unlocked with a *click.*

A large bed with crisp, white sheets and pillows. A TV attached to the wall. No kitchen facilities. Bottled water, a pre-packaged sandwich and a net of tangerines on a small table pushed up against the wall. A tall wardrobe was open. Blankets were folded on the high shelves, five plastic coat hangers hung from a rod and an ironing board stood on end. The bathroom was tiny yet functional and smelt of cleaning fluid. It was like a clean two-star hotel.

So this is where he would wait out the apocalypse?

***

Static interrupted some of the reporting on the radio. They must have been in an area with limited reception.

Gemma played with the dial. She knew the government manipulated the release of information. They did exactly that during the Aberdeen breakout. The world did not know for days. But whatever slice of information she could receive was better than none.

"Areas to avoid, Aberdeen and the surrounding areas."

"Bastards," she whispered. "Old news."

"Quarantine was breached and infected are moving outside the city limits. The Civilian Assistance Force is redeploying and communities are being evacuated. Outbreaks are reported in Edinburgh, Glasgow, Dundee, Perth and Inverness. Government officials advise to remain where you are, and wait—"

More static.

"Let me try." Jacob leaned across.

She slapped at his hand. "Concentrate on the road!"

They travelled around a blind bend. Smoking metal and twisted car bodies blocked the road.

"Watch out!"

Jacob slammed on the breaks.

"What's happened? A fire of some kind?" he suggested.

"An airstrike," said Gemma. "Look, you can see the scorch marks from the blast."

"Jesus, no!" Jacob unbuckled his seatbelt.

"What are you doing?"

"Bodies! Those are people!"

"No, Jacob. If they were blown up from an airstrike, it was for good reason."

Jacob ignored her warning and jumped out of the car.

"Is anyone alive?" Jacob called out.

"Shit," Gemma said to no one. She knew what was coming. She had seen it before, too many times. Gemma climbed across and into the driver's seat. She opened the window. "Get in," she called as quietly as she could.

"Hello? We can help if there's anyone there."

"Jacob, you're about to be a dead man. Get in."

Far beyond the wreckages, up on the banks, shadows appeared.

"You get in now, or you're on your own."

"What are they?"

Gemma revved the car. That had Jacob limping as fast as he could. He climbed in.

The infected were on the move. They fell down the embankment, righted themselves and charged. Gemma slipped the car into reverse, accelerated and headed back the way they'd come.

"They're following!" screamed Jacob.

"No shit!"

"They're coming fast."

"They always do. Buckle up."

"I was trying to help. There could have been someone out there injured."

"Learn a lesson. Next time, listen to me."

"Sure," he said meekly.

"We had soldiers to pull the trigger back in the hospital, but now, it's just you and me. So we *do not* play Good Samaritan when it's obvious the infected are close by. Got it?"

"I said yes, didn't I? We need to pull over somewhere and figure out where we should go."

"We're heading back south, back toward the hospital."

"Why?"

She didn't reply.

"Do you have a plan?"

"No."

"No?"

"The next city heading south is Dundee. We should avoid it, if possible."

"Maybe we should get off the main roads?"

"That's what I'm trying to do."

"Can we do something about food and drink? I've not eaten for hours."

Five miles later they reached a turnoff, little more than a minor road, but it took them off the arterial motorway. Ahead, the road turned into a serpentine challenge. Driving conditions were poor. They drove in silence, pulling further away from the dangers of the main roads. In all the years Gemma lived in Aberdeen, she had no cause to explore some of the more remote towns and villages around the city, so this was all alien to her. She was sure eventually they would come to some kind of population centre, somewhere they could find supplies and perhaps information. What she wanted to avoid was arriving at a large town that could be gripped by infection.

Ahead came the reassuring glow of street lights. A cluster of houses spanned either side of the road, the type of hamlet that Gemma would normally drive through without sparring a second thought. But here, she studied everything. She looked for signs of life. Indications that she was being watched. Anything to suggest she was not alone. Where had the people gone? Were they dead inside or one of the numberless infected stalking the world.

On the far side were six houses. On their side, two houses and a small shop that also served as a post office. All the houses were in darkness, curtains closed, no sign of activity.

"Looks quiet enough." Gemma turned the engine off. "The infected don't have the lights and TV on. Looks safe until they come running out of the dark."

Jacob leaned forward. "Look at the shop. The door is open, right? It's not just me that see's that?"

"Seems like it," said Gemma. "Someone could have broken into the shop."

"Saves us the trouble then, doesn't it?"

"Follow my lead. If I say stop, you stop."

"I can take care of myself."

"Don't be cocky. One bad move and I'm in trouble too. So be smart or you might not live to make a second mistake."

They both got out of the car. Gemma pulled on her backpack, and they walked toward the shop. The wind blew over them with ruthless force. Gemma touched a hand to the knife stashed down her boot. She'd get to it quickly if the need presented itself.

The door of the shop was open, the lights off inside. Pinned to the frame of the door, a hand written note, secured inside a plastic pocket.

Jacob wiped his hand over the face of the sheet.

Take only what you need. Be safe. Be generous. God bless.

He poked his head through the threshold.

"It's dark but it looks empty."

Jacob stepped into the shop, his feet crunching on broken glass, and made a lot of noise as he made his way through the shelves.

Gemma waited.

"It's a mess," he said.

The infected reacted to noise instantly, but Gemma sensed no movement.

"You coming in?" he asked.

She waited a little more, then peeked inside. Still no sign of any infected. She stepped in. The shelves were tightly placed. Much of the stock was depleted or missing. Empty packets littered the floor. Beyond the shop, the post office annex was locked up, a secured gate blocking access to it.

"Be quick," she said. "Take what you can then we head back to the car."

"We could turn the lights on."

"No. No lights."

"Well, don't blame me if I grab something past its date."

"You grab something past its date, and it's yours."

Gemma bent low. On the bottom shelf she found three bottles of water and two bottles of soda.

The blow to the back of her head came so quickly, it sent her sprawling across the floor. She rolled ready to fight off the infected. Jacob stood over her, a can held high in his hand.

"Don't try get up or I'll hit you again."

"You bastard," she said feeling the gash at the back of her head.

"Yeah maybe. But I'm taking the car and leaving. It's nothing personal. In the hospital I needed you. Now I don't."

Gemma's hand moved to her boot.

"No, no, no you don't." Jacob leant in closer with the can. She stilled.

"You go for that knife, and the next hit will send you to la la land."

"Why are you doing this?"

"It's all about survival. What you said to me at the wrecks about helping people, you're right, I don't know you. You could be planning to get rid of me when the moment is right. I intend to live a long and happy life. So I'm starting right now. Goodbye, Gemma. You take care now."

Jacob left. Moments later the car started and the lights briefly lit up the windows.

Gemma touched at her wound and brought her fingers to her face. Blood.

"You're an idiot, Gemma."

She stood, and held onto the shelf as dizziness came and went.

"Who'd have thought he had it in him?" she said to the shelves. "What to do now?"

No car. No phone. No Black Aquila to help. Information that did her little good.

Gemma closed the door, blocking out the night. With the door closed, it felt warmer. Or at least she told herself that. The till tray on the counter was open but empty. A small plug-in bar heater sat in the corner. She clicked it on. A cheery orange glow and welcome heat pumped out. In the morning, she would look for a first-aid kit to clean and dress her forehead. After that she would look to making her way. Where? She did not know.

***

"What do you think?" asked Brutus.

"I think you're crazy but you know that," answered Niall.

Lying flat in the damp, on the roof of a building, they could study Brutus's target through binoculars.

"We used a lot of ammo getting here," said Niall. "The creatures won't be content to stay within the city centre. They'll spread outwards soon."

"That's why we need to work quickly. Looks like this place isn't fully functioning yet. So we either need to go now before they beef up security, or we come up with another plan. Our options are slipping away by the second."

Niall lowered his binoculars. "Have you ever read about Richard the Lionheart? He crusaded to capture Jerusalem and when he finally reached the walls of the city, he realised he needed to turn back. He didn't have the troops or the resources to survive a lengthy siege."

"Thank you, Professor History."

"We're a small team. If we take it, we can hold it. But what happens to the people already there? Do we force them to leave? Are they collateral? Do we try to work out an arrangement?"

"You sound like you care."

Niall shrugged. "Contingencies only. Don't read more into it than that."

"We can take it, fast and quiet. After that, we decide what to do."

Brutus and Niall moved from their observation point and returned to the van.

The team had arrived. Ash Gibbons, Roy Smart, Magnus Munson, Freddo McLeod and Stuart Taylor. They stood at the roadside strapping on their gear.

"I've shot out the surrounding streetlights. Will give us a concealed approach," announced Brutus.

"Other security? External cameras?" asked Roy.

"There's more cameras stuck on that building than I could count. I shot one out and waited. Nobody came to investigate. My guess is they're not monitored. Not yet at least. So I took them all out. Still nothing. Our approach is secure."

"You've been busy," said Roy, nodding.

"More than you know. Murray, take the families into this office building." Brutus indicated an address on a map. "They can wait it out there. We're going in soon."

Magnus Munson sat in the back of the van checking the mechanisms of the AK-47s. "What are we facing, Brutus?"

"Full complement of staff and residents has not arrived yet. We go in fast and clean. Roy will be on the roof of the office block over there, and you'll take out the four sentries on the walls. We make our way to the gate, fight our way in, secure the courtyard and proceed inside. Once we have the hallway, we'll move floor to floor, sweeping as we go. I expect unarmed civilians, but at the first sign of trouble, take them out."

"We're wasting time here," said Freddo. "Let's do this."

"Roy, take position."

Roy slung his Russian-made sniper rifle over his shoulder and dashed off.

Magnus screwed suppressors to each rifle and handed them out. "Four magazines and three grenades each. But remember that's our new home."

"Niall," said Brutus, "once we're inside the perimeter I want you on the walls."

Niall nodded.

Brutus stuffed the magazines into his tac vest, securing them in the pouches. He slotted a fifth magazine into the weapon and made it ready.

The team looked a little nervous, and with good reason. If they were to fail here the options were limited in what they could do next. The infected were sure to arrive before long.

"Okay, boys. Time to move. Fast, silent and hard. You know how we work."

Magnus closed the side door of the van and readied his weapon.

Brutus led the five men. They hugged the walls of the buildings, holding to the shadows. It made him smile as he imagined the chaos to come.

Rain was falling. They reached a warehouse and Brutus raised a hand. His team halted.

"From here, we turn left, down a side street and right. We'll come out at the edge of the wall. We wait for Roy to take the sentries on the wall, then we proceed parallel to the wall, reach the gate, take out the three sentries on the gate. Remember, no radios for now."

Brutus set off again, his team a step behind. They splashed through puddles and rounded the corner. The side street was little more than waste ground between two walls of the warehouse. Thick and overgrown with weeds, the ground turned at hidden angles beneath the green. Brutus reached a chain-link fence at the end. He cupped his hands and boosted each member of his team up and over the fence. Brutus followed them over.

They remained crouched, covered by the shadow of the building. Brutus crept to the corner of the building. The wall was fifty metres ahead. Brutus pulled his binoculars free and scanned the rooftop for Roy. If Brutus had not known where to look, he could have spent hours searching the similar rooftops for the sniper. Roy knew his craft well.

Roy was looking directly to where Brutus and his team gathered through his spotter binoculars.

There was a grunt, and a sentry fell from the wall, clattering to the pavement below. The metallic ring of his weapon held in the air.

Roy signalled four times with a small flashlight. The last guard on the wall to be neutralised was the one closest to them. Stuart Taylor scooped up the fallen weapon and put the strap over his shoulder.

Brutus waved the team forward, making a dash to the wall. They reached it in a single breath. Brutus threw his back against the hard concrete. He shouldered the AK-47 and moved again. The entrance neared. At the cusp of the wall Brutus slowed and crouched.

Without radios they would do it the old fashion way. Act and react.

The forecourt was not a particularly well-lit area. The little light came from floodlights set further back from the gate. Brutus popped his head past the threshold. Three guards, armed. Standing together in quiet conversation. Not one looked out past the boundary of the wall. He pulled himself back. Brutus raised a hand with three fingers extended and motioned that they stood on the right of the gate, then signalled that Niall, Taylor and himself would take the three guards down.

Brutus counted to three silently then stepped round the corner into the gateway, weapon raised. He sensed his team moving with him, a well-rehearsed machine.

None of the guards were aware of the approaching danger. Brutus squeezed off two silent shots. His target jerked back, clutching his neck and fell to the ground. He thrashed on the ground. Niall and Taylor's targets fell without a sound. Brutus stepped over the dead and fired two shots into the chest of his target. The thrashing ceased. He swore at himself, angered at his inaccurate shooting. Especially when Niall and Taylor shot like master marksmen.

Loading crews who dealt with the deliveries were sitting off to the far left. They huddled against the rain under a thin canopy. Brutus waved Magnus to round them up. Freddo went with him.

"Hey, you guys! Over here."

Magnus approached, not with his weapon raised but with a hand raised in salute. He let his weapon fall to its sling but kept his other hand on it. Freddo stood just behind, weapon ready but not aimed.

They turned to the newcomers, not overly alarmed.

"Who's in charge here?" asked Magnus.

An older man, clad in a reflective vest and hardhat stepped from the group. "I'm the foreman. Is there some kind of problem?"

"There's been some issues, we're going to need you and your boys to stay in a contained area until it's resolved."

Freddo stepped past Magnus. He raised his weapon at the group of men. "In fact, how's about you all get down on your knees. Hands on your head, and now."

Magnus's weapon was up, too.

The foreman raised his hands, and stepped back to be with the group. "Do as they say."

"Wise," said Freddo, shouldering his weapon and removing ties from his vest.

Brutus brought his weapon around and opened fire on the kneeling men.

"Jesus!" Freddo stepped back, checking himself for blood spatters. "Did you have to do that right now?"

Brutus reloaded his weapon and stuck an unlit cigar in his mouth. A thud came, and a guard slipped down the steps, leaving a trail of blood on the concrete steps. Roy, the guardian up high, proved his reputation right.

"So far so good," Niall said. "I'm going up the wall. We still don't know how many of them are in there."

Brutus nodded. "We're good to proceed."

They moved past the dead guard, weapons raised, and took the steps. Indoors and out of the rain felt like another world. Brutus had become used to the constant downpour. The reception was empty. Terminals and office furnishings had been installed. No staff. It reminded Brutus of the hospital in Aberdeen. It was as if a force removed all humans from the facility; one moment there, the next gone.

Movement caught his eye on the mezzanine. A figure moved at the cusp of the barrier, a head appearing for a second before ducking back to cover.

"Get to cover!" Brutus threw himself right and slid across the floor, finding cover behind a column. A high powered weapon opened up from above. Rounds slammed into the masonry where Brutus sought shelter. Freddo angled himself from behind a row of seats and returned fire. Taylor waved to Brutus and pointed to the grenades on his vest. Brutus shook his head. He wanted to avoid damage to the building, as much as possible. More gunfire ripped through the vestibule, shattering seats and desks. Freddo's cover was eroding.

"Get yourself out of there," said Brutus.

"Cover me!" shouted Freddo.

Brutus slipped from behind the column and sent five rounds upwards at the unseen enemy.

Freddo scrambled from the floor, slipping on shell casings, then regained his footing and sprinted to Brutus. Brutus fired two shots and stepped back next to Freddo.

"Got any ideas?"

"One. Hey," he called out. "You guys up on the balcony. Time to talk."

A round of gunfire erupted in response. Brutus was not surprised. He waited for the echo to subside.

"Are we going to spend the morning shooting at each other? Nobody else needs to die here today. I'm offering you a way out of all this."

"Doesn't look to me that we need a way out of here," said a voice from above. "We can hold this point indefinitely. We're in no rush to go anywhere."

"About that, I wonder how much food you have up there, how much ammunition. Killing more of you doesn't fill me with joy," he lied. "You are simply an obstacle to my objective. I'm giving you a choice. Free passage out of here or die defending something you have no interest in."

The silence that followed was encouraging.

"How do we know we can trust you?" asked the voice.

"Trust is earned, my friend. If we do this, I meet you face to face. You have my word that none of my men will fire on you. But I need more from you."

"Such as?"

"How many men do you have?"

"You think me stupid?" snapped the faceless soldier.

"Come on, now. That's not fostering trust. My patience is limited. How many men?"

That hesitation came again.

"There's ten of us and three managers upstairs."

Yes, I think you stupid, Brutus said to himself. "Who are the managers?"

"The ones in charge of the building. Two men and a female."

One more than Brutus guessed.

"Here's what you're going to do, my friend. You're going to secure the managers in restraints and bring them down to the lobby. You'll store your weapons and my men will escort you out of the building and to the city. There, your weapons will be given back on the condition that you never return here. There will be no further terms. You accept them or you die."

"You'll give us time to consider the offer?"

"Ten minutes. If we don't hear from you within that time, we're coming in hot."

The rest of the team waited, weapons ready.

"What do you think?" said Brutus.

Freddo inspected a thick splinter of wood protruding from his forearm, then pulled it free. "I think we've a shot at getting this place without a bloodbath."

"Yeah, if we have to kill them it'll get messy."

"Hey! Are you there?"

"I'm here," replied Brutus.

"Let's have a face to face. I'll come down the stairs. No weapons. My men won't fire as long as yours don't."

"Sounds good."

Taylor shook his head, cautioning against such a move.

Brutus nodded. It was going to happen, no matter the protest. He removed his AK-47 and handed it to Freddo, then pulled his Glock from the holster at his leg and tucked it down the back of his trousers.

Heavy footsteps thumped down the stairs. A figure rounded the stairwell and descended the last few steps. He waited at the bottom, his hands open at his sides. The soldier wore the same uniform as those outside.

Brutus stepped out from his cover. Above on the mezzanine more of the security team watched, still hugging cover. Brutus's boots crunched on shell casings. Off to his left, behind a row of seats offered the best cover if he needed to opt out of the face to face. Both men walked toward each other until they met in the middle of the lobby. No man's land.

The soldier stood several inches shorter than Brutus. He was bald with a trimmed beard more white than dark. He had the look of a weary soldier, too long on deployment.

"Who would have thought the person responsible for killing my men would be a face from my past?"

"I sure as hell don't remember you," said Brutus.

"No? Funny how fate throws people together. A time ago we stood on the same side of the line. Now, as the world changes, we find ourselves as opposing forces."

"A goddamned philosopher," said Brutus.

The soldier gave a gruff laugh. "Don't all soldiers who have seen what you and I have seen turn such a way in the end?"

"You speak in riddles. Not wise when negotiating for your life."

"And I thought I was conversing with an old companion."

"The offer still stands for the moment. Free passage. Supplies and transport for you and your men. In return, you leave here and never come back. And the managers stay."

"I'm wondering as we stand here speaking what do you want with the managers. Surely you have everything you want here already?"

"One last time. The offer stands. Take it or leave it."

"Is it as bad as I suspect out there?"

"Getting worse by the minute."

"This will become a place of death, Brutus. The people you've gone to war with, they won't allow you to take what's theirs. But I think you know this, no?"

"You have my word."

"My men have orders to hold position for the moment until my return. Perhaps we can take a walk to the motor pool? I can select a vehicle?"

The soldier was enigmatic and confident, while relying on some past familiarity. Perhaps Brutus was incorrect to label him stupid. Better to assume him capable.

"If you're men attempt to move from their position they will be fired upon."

"Nobody else needs to die here today," said the soldier, echoing the words of Brutus.

***

Explosions far off rumbled and lit the morning sky like fireworks. Ryan stood naked and watched from his window, his lights out. Aircraft dropped ordinance over the buildings across the river, the brilliance of each attack reflected in a hundred windows. A war was being fought in London, and the Owl's made their nest at the heart of it.

Ryan drained a bottle of water and let it fall to the floor. Three urgent knocks came at the door. Ryan pulled on a shirt and his jeans. He crossed to the door, found the light switch and opened the door.

Hector Crispin pushed past Ryan.

"Close the door."

Ryan never knew how to address Hector correctly. Mr. Nippon? Hector? Mr. Crispin? Whatever name Ryan used it felt incorrect. He wondered if he would ever get over being nervous around the man.

Hector's top button was undone and his tie loosened to over causal.

"Hello, um, Mr. Crispin. I was hoping you would seek me out."

"How do you like our magnificent work?" He spread his arms wide.

Ryan didn't respond, feeling the question to be rhetorical. Hector crossed to the window and gazed out at the city. His gait told Ryan the man was drunk.

"All the years of planning. A generation of preparation. Millions of dollars sunk into this project, every detail considered, contingency plans put into place. The very culmination is this point and do you know what I was told not two hours ago?" He turned.

Ryan opened his hands. "I have no—"

"Glasgow Sanctuary is behind schedule! The residents are in transit to the facility through a city rapidly being consumed by the Carrion Virus. Behind schedule! We cannot fail in this, Ryan. Your father dedicated his life to this cause. We have to succeed." Hector sat heavily on the bed. "And are we doing anything to address the situation?"

"We?"

Hector frowned. "Of course, we." He gestured to every corner of the room.

"Well, I'm not sure, sir."

When did The Owls of Athena and Ryan become *we*? Probably around the same time he realised his survival depended on them entirely. He never liked the group. Never liked the idea of the group. He had simply been swept up in it all, excited about an adventure, foregoing the warning that tapped at his conscience in the niggling form of fear.

"Last progress we received suggested they were a few hours away. There is a hostile city for them to battle through yet, and it won't be easy."

"Is there something I can help with, Hector, I mean, Mr. Crispin?"

He blew out his cheeks and returned to the window. He swayed slightly. "Not the auspicious start we were hoping for. Information from the world at large is difficult to come by. We believe hostilities have broken out between Indian and Pakistani forces. I imagined when the enemy of mankind arose, the notion of butchering each other would fall by the wayside. But no. Two nuclear-armed powers skirmishing at the border, while the infected devour their cities. The Owls of Athena have ushered in a new period of madness. As brief as it will be, humanity will continue to stupefy me."

"Can I get you some water, Mr. Crispin, sir?" Ryan picked up his empty bottle from the floor and threw it in the rubbish bin. He wanted to enquire as to whether recycling was undertaken in the building. Perhaps one of his fellow travellers was a recycling expert. They couldn't allow rubbish to build up in a place like this, could they? The stench would soon climb to be uncomfortable then disgusting then choking. But he thought it best to leave such a question to later. Maybe he'd discover for himself.

"You will hear gunfire soon. Close. Defensive fire. Formations of infected have been spotted not far off. There's no effective resistance in this part of the city other than us. Our gates are barred. Let us hope they hold. I expect this will be a daily occurrence from now."

"Mr. Hector, sir, Mr. Crispin?"

Hector turned appearing startled, as if he just became aware of Ryan. "Yes, Ryan?"

"The sanctuary is very close to the centre of the city. We'll be surrounded by the infected soon, no?"

"You think it was an ill-advised move?"

"I ... I wouldn't presume to know the thinking of people more intelligent and influential than me."

"Being surrounded by infected is only dangerous for those who aren't prepared. And having a hostile city surrounding us provides protection from elements who might wish to do us harm. We hide in plain sight, among the afflicted."

"Oh, I understand," said Ryan.

"I doubt that very much," said Hector matter-of-factly. "You should get some sleep. Tomorrow will be a busy day. The first official operational day."

"I would like to talk again, sometime soon?"

"A great number of matters will require my attention. And I am sure you will be kept busy."

"Doing what? I mean, Mr. Crispin, may I ask what my role is here?"

Hector smiled and did a bad job of straightening his tie. "You'll find out soon enough. Get some rest, my friend. Tomorrow is a new day in a new world. A new day in a new world," he repeated before stepping out the door and closing it behind him.

***

The car pool felt like a concrete tomb, cavernous and burrowed beneath the ground level. It boasted a fuel pump and small off-road dirt bikes, cycles, 4X4s, electric cars, a small bus that could seat fifteen, and a heavily modified Land Rover with armour plating. To the rear of the chamber was a machine shop for repairs and alterations.

"You've not asked my name," said the soldier, his voice echoing in the concrete vault.

"No."

"It's Silas Salt."

The name, unusual and familiar still escaped Brutus, but he said nothing.

"What about the loaders you've got under guard?"

"None of your concern," said Brutus. "You can take the minibus. Where are the keys?"

Silas pointed to a small cabin by the ramp leading up and out of the underground lair.

"Get the keys."

"As you wish," said Silas.

Brutus followed his every move. Silas snatched the keys from the cabin.

"Back to the hallway. To your men," ordered Brutus.

Silas opened his mouth but closed it before words spilled. They returned to the main building and shook off rain that caught them between the subterranean vault and the entrance.

Brutus waved Taylor over. "The garage's out the front door and down. There's a minibus. Bring it up front and leave the engine running."

Silas handed over the keys. Taylor headed off to do as ordered, and Freddo handed Brutus his weapon.

"Tell your men to pile your weapons at the top of the stairs, then with hands on heads they're to come down the stairs. They'll be searched before boarding the minibus. Your men first, then we'll collect the managers and you're last."

Silas nodded then climbed the stairs. Brutus pulled his handgun from the back of his trousers and slid it back to his leg holster.

"He says he knows me," Brutus said to Freddo.

"Do you know him?"

"I don't think so. Maybe."

"What's his name," asked Freddo.

"Silas Salt."

Freddo scratched at his head. "I've not heard of him."

"Well we won't need to worry about them for much longer." Brutus stroked his beard. The wound on his face burned. He patted it, expecting to discover that it seeped. He'd dispatched the author of the newer cut, and if he ever caught that bitch who created the older cut she would pay, that's if she wasn't already dead. And that was more than likely. Aberdeen was a dangerous place.

Taylor pulled up outside the lobby in the minibus and threw Brutus a thumbs up.

Brutus briefed his men on the evacuation process and they moved into place.

"Silas?" he called out.

"Yes?" Silas appeared at the lip of the mezzanine wall.

"Start sending your men down, one at a time."

Silas moved out of view.

The first soldier appeared, his arms on his head, his steps down the stairs orderly and controlled. He reached the bottom step.

"Far enough," said Ash Gibbons. Ash patted the man down with a practiced hand while Taylor aimed his firearm at the man's head.

The soldier's eyes did not move from Taylor's trigger finger.

"Clear," announced Ash, and the soldier was waved to the entrance door.

Number seven of the ten security detail marched past Brutus. He walked with his fists balled, arms rigid to his side.

"Hand's on head, asshole," Brutus warned, his weapon aimed.

The soldier ignored Brutus's warning and upon reaching Taylor threw a shoulder into him. Brutus reached them as Taylor

98

drew his sidearm. At close range Brutus fired a single round into the soldier's neck. The shot rang out, the impact of the bullet almost tearing the soldier's head clean off. He fell forward. Dead.

Taylor spun and aimed his handgun at those in the minibus. "Make a move and you're dead, too. All of you."

Brutus kicked the body over. "Anyone else tries something like this and you'll be lying next to him." He marched back into the building, leaving Taylor outside to cover them.

Silas watched from the upper level, grasping the rail. He shook his head but said nothing to Brutus.

"Send the next one down," ordered Brutus.

The rest of the security team were processed without incident.

Silas came back down the stairs. "That's the lot of them. Just me left. Would you care to inspect the weapons and managers?"

Brutus looked to the stairs. Silas could have lied, have double the men and set up an ambush. Somehow he doubted it. "Stay here. I'll call for you."

Brutus waved Ash to guard Silas. He climbed the stairs, reaching the upper level, and there stood the pile of weapons: MP5s, pistols and magazines. Further along the corridor that lead away from the overhang of the upper level, three people knelt. Their hands were secured behind their backs, black bags over their heads. They appeared to be wearing nightwear. One of the men was topless. The other wore a plain grey shirt. The female was wrapped in a housecoat, thin and see through it left little to the imagination. Even from the distance Brutus could see they breathed quickly.

He crossed to the wall and looked out over the lobby. "Send Silas up."

Ash pushed Silas Salt toward the stairs. He laughed, only a little, only enough to irritate Ash who moved to punish him but Brutus raised a hand.

Freddo now stood with Taylor guarding the minibus. The driver's seat was still empty. No doubt Roy watched everything unfold and would take a shot if he felt the situation necessitated action.

Silas reached the top step and walked onto the upper level toward Brutus. He swept a hand down to the pile of weapons and ammunition. "As promised. The men expect safe conduct from the building and some means of protection returned to them."

"Join your men and leave."

"I'm not going."

"Trust me, you're going. One way or another you'll be leaving this place. I don't much care how."

"You need me." Silas crossed his arms. "You need me more than you know."

Brutus laughed this time. "I don't need you. I have them." He pointed to the three restrained managers. "Anything I need they will tell me."

"And if they won't talk?"

"Getting people to talk has never been something I struggled with."

"You need me," he said again.

"I'm done talking, Silas. You and your men will leave now." He felt like launching Silas from the mezzanine.

"What if I had something to show you?"

"I'm not interested." But he was. He was always interested in information. Brutus stepped closer to Silas.

"What I have to show you might just make the difference between you holding onto this place, and you and your men being dead within twenty-four hours."

"You have five minutes, Silas. For your sake, don't waste any of it."

"Then follow me."

Brutus leaned over the barrier and signed that he would be back in five minutes and pulled the Glock from his leg holster.

Silas lead the way through the main corridor of the first floor. Each door was uniformed in pale wooden panelling, most probably reinforced with metal, the keycard scanners lit by a single, red light. They reached a door at the end of the corridor. Silas turned. Brutus raised the pistol.

"You won't need that, I promise."

"Prove it."

Silas pulled a keycard attached to his belt by a cord and extended it to the door scanner. The light blinked from red to green and the lock opened with a *click.*

"Here we are." Silas opened the door, swinging it wide.

Brutus stepped back and aimed the Glock at Silas.

***

Something woke Eric. A morning noise? A dream? He was not sure. The fire glowed, the embers giving one final effort before succumbing. Skye snored softly. He climbed out of bed. His head pounded. While rest healed his body, it also made him weak and stiff. He moved clumsily. His freshly washed and ironed clothes sat neatly piled on a chair. Skye moved from the bed, her front paws extended out in a stretch. She yawned and padded over to Eric giving his hand a lick. He dressed and left the bedroom. Every light in the house was off. The house was silent except for the ticking of a clock somewhere. The room felt cluttered. Every few steps brought another obstacle to feel his way around. He reached the front door and opened it as quietly as possible. Skye gave a whimper at being left in the house.

The coming sun, still below the horizon, provided a little light to the landscape. Snow fell irregularly, not a heavy shower but enough to remind people that winter was far from over in rural Scotland. The temperature must have been somewhere below freezing and minus five. Eric's breath misted. Footprints in the snow led off to the right and around the side of the house. He followed them for the moment, with no real idea of why he was outside other than the sense that something could be wrong.

"Jesus!" Allan appeared from around the corner, his shotgun in hand. "What are you doing out here?"

"I heard a noise and thought to come out here to make sure everything was okay. I didn't expect to find you."

"Is Hazel alright?" he asked with urgency.

"I don't know."

"She didn't wake?"

"Not that I know of. What's going on?"

"Follow me."

Allan led Eric away from the house, toward the outbuildings, his rifle pointing downwards. He reached into a shed and pulled out an old jacket, thick and waterproof. Dried mud caked the material. He threw it to Eric.

"Thanks."

"You need to promise me that you won't say a thing to Hazel. She's a gentle woman. A kind woman, you understand? What I don't tell her, I do out of love. She wouldn't understand. But you, lad. I think you might understand all too well. And I think you may have some ideas."

They crunched through the snow.

"What is it you think I understand, Mr. Ingram?"

"You know how the world is now. There's been a change. I don't claim to understand it. I listen to the radio. And I watched the TV before it went dead. It's things. Society is breaking down. Worse than that. And I suspect you've been exposed to it."

Eric didn't respond.

"Out here, I thought we would be safe from the worst of it. We've always been left to our own devices. Nobody to bother us. The neighbours we've known most of our lives. Nothing changes here. Until the last while, I suppose. When I found you, out in the snow, collapsed and dying of cold it wasn't by chance."

Allan breathed heavier. The wind blew with a renewed vigour. They reached the last building on the farm, a large concrete barn with a metal roof. The steel door was secured with a heavy-duty padlock.

"What do you mean it wasn't by chance?"

Allan leaned on the wall of the barn. The cold did not seem to bother him. He was a large man, withered by age but looked to be from hardworking, farming stock.

"The farm has long since been a working farm. Now, we have a small amount of animals, mostly for old times' sake. We don't see many visitors out here. Not even our neighbours. A couple of days before you arrived, Skye was going berserk barking at our window, and scratching at the door. It wasn't like her. I went out with her, and not far from the house I saw someone in the field. I called out to them. He ran at me. Eric, I didn't know what was wrong with him. He threw himself at me, lad. Didn't even pause to think about it."

"Did it hurt you?" *How many days have I been here?*

"No, I put him down. I've been shooting shotguns since I was a lad. I called the police after I shot him and reported being attacked. They took my name and what happened but advised they could not provide me with a response time. What police force doesn't have time to attend a shooting? It told me a lot. So, Eric, these people, what are they?"

"What happened when you shot it? Tell me exactly."

Allan tapped a finger at the wall he leaned against. "Why does it matter now? It's done. Nothing's going to change that."

"It's important."

"Like I said, it came charging at me. I had my gun with me. Until it got close, I didn't realise something was terribly wrong. It launched itself at me. I pushed it back with the gun. I shouted out, warning him not to come closer. It charged again and I fired."

"Did it touch you? Scrape you with its nails? What about the blood? Did you get any on you?"

"No. Why?"

"It's called Carrion Virus. Once someone has fully succumbed to the virus they're changed in a way. They become violent, frenzied. They don't communicate like before. They develop unnatural strength. They're resistant to injury. They can't be reasoned with. You were lucky, Mr. Ingram. Most people are overcome by their strength, and the virus is passed on. Bites. Scratches. Contamination through blood or excessive contact."

"You've dealt with them before?"

"I was in Aberdeen when the initial outbreak occurred. I've been combating them in one place or another since."

"You're army? Police?"

"Something like that."

Allan smiled. "Five minutes with you out in the morning snow and I know more about what's going on than I did from hours with the radio. You can help me with something, Eric."

Allan unlocked the barn door and pulled the heavy metal barrier open.

Inside, laid out on the concrete floor were five bodies. All were covered with old sheets, the kind that painters might use to protect furniture.

Allan pointed to the nearest shroud. "That one I shot just before you came outside. She was wandering in the field. I don't think she noticed me until it was too late." The farmer shook his head. "And those there are two of my neighbours. I've known them for thirty years. I didn't know what to do with the bodies. The cold is keeping them for now but they can't stay in my barn for much longer. When the weather eases, Hazel will be outside again. She can't see this."

Eric stepped into the barn. "Burn them."

"I don't think we could start a fire in this weather."

"How hard's the ground?"

Allan pointed to tools leaning against the wall of the barn. "Nothing a bit of effort won't combat. How's your ribs?"

"We'll find out."

"We can park the tractor over the graves."

Shovels and picks swung as the sun began to rise and despite the cold both men sweated. Eric swore more than once, and took breaks to allow the pain to dissipate. But together they achieved, and they tossed the bodies into the new trench.

"I feel like I should say something," said Allan. "It doesn't feel right what's happened to them."

***

Eric and Allan walked back toward the farmhouse.

"There's a lot of outbuildings around here. Do you check them regularly?" asked Eric.

Allan nodded, reached out and touched the large shed closest to them. "The ones I don't need to go in and out of I keep locked. I've got my motor in here. I've not needed it for a while. Most of the other buildings are locked. When I take Skye out we check all the doors to make sure they've not been tampered with."

"Sensible. You're doing well here."

"We manage," said Allan.

They continued on.

Skye barked from the house.

"Something's wrong. Skye's not much of a barker for no reason."

Allan ran to the house and Eric followed. Allan threw the door open.

"No!" Allan screamed.

Hazel lay face down on the floor, her arms stretched out ahead as if she had tripped and tried to soften the fall. She bled from wounds on her back and arms and calves.

"Don't touch her!"

Allan ignored the warning, tossed his gun aside and fell to his knees beside his dead wife. He rolled her over, pulled her to his chest and stroked her hair.

Skye barked in the direction of the kitchen. An infected appeared in a doorway. Its blue ski jacket and furry boots were stained and torn. It wore one glove. Eric snatched up Allan's shotgun, aimed and pulled the trigger. The shot ripped its chest apart, and threw it backwards landing on the small breakfast table. Plates and cutlery tumbled to the floor. Eric checked the second barrel. Loaded. He walked to the infected. Nothing remained of its chest. It didn't need a second bullet.

Allan hadn't moved. He held his wife tightly and wept quietly in between whispered words.

Eric knew it was only a matter of time before another infected appeared.

"Allan?"

"I'm not leaving her."

"I know."

Allan looked up to Eric. "You know what to do. Look after Skye." His focus returned to his dead wife. He began singing softly. It was a lovely tune. Perhaps one the couple danced too often, one that was important to them, held memories.

"What are you waiting for?" said Allan, breaking from the song. He pulled Hazel close and closed his eyes.

Eric fired.

***

The Ingram's Land Rover wasn't keen to start. It took Eric three goes, and all the while Skye sat next to him, his head dipping side to side, his ears pointing to the sky. In the foot well, a backpack with Eric's firearms and those few things he risked time to grab. They reached the roadway. Figures appeared in the snow and charged their way toward them. They all wore the same blue ski jacket and furry boots. Where were they coming from?

Eric drove from out behind the shelter of the farmhouse. He drove fast. Infected threw themselves at the vehicle and bounced off. Eric kept his speed up, turning a tight corner and passing through the farm's gate. In the mirror he could see the pursuing infected slowing and gathering and turning their attention to a new direction.

Eric and Skye had escaped that onslaught, but there was sure to be more ahead. Lots more. He hit the heating, sending a welcome blast of warmth at his face. Skye lifted her head and sniffed before settling back down.

"We're right for the moment, girl."

He was glad of the company. The road ahead would be difficult, and full of danger but somehow the dog made the prospect all the more bearable.

***

The room was rancid with the choking aroma of death, shit and piss. Brutus slammed Silas into the wall and thrust the barrel of his Glock under his chin.

"Start talking, Silas. Otherwise you're a dead man."

Silas did not appear too concerned. He gave Brutus a moment of attention then looked over his shoulder into the room.

The original purpose of the room may once have been for storage, perhaps a deposit for old records, but nothing of importance. It was neither impressive nor strategically designed. But now, it was a murder room. Corpses were piled atop each other in two piles a couple of feet apart. Fourteen in all, each with a cut throat. Blood painted the floor and walls. All wore the uniform of the facility's security detail.

Brutus pushed the weapon harder into his neck. "Talk!"

"Don't you understand? That is the price for your kingdom, Brutus. You want this building. There were those within the security team who wanted to fight and not negotiate. These are the ones who the facility managers, your managers, relied on the most. I simply removed them from the scenario. The person you first negotiated with is dead behind you. When I took action, I took control."

"What do you want, Silas? No games. No cryptic messages."

"I want to stay here. I've fought the infected and I've no desire to return to that life again."

"What makes you think I would allow you to stay here?"

"You need me."

"You've given me nothing. I'm inclined to say no."

Brutus holstered his Glock then threw a short punch into Silas's stomach. Silas doubled over. Brutus brought his knee up into his nose. A bone cracked. Silas slid to the ground, his hands climbing to his face.

"You jerked me around, Silas. You get nothing. I could kill you and add our body to one of those piles, and I'd not think twice about it."

"Ah, yet here you are, thinking twice. If I wanted to kill you, Brutus, I could have done it at any time. See?" A dark blade appeared in his hand. He dropped it, left is palm open, and spat blood to the side.

Brutus kicked the blade away, hauled Silas to his feet, and pushed the barrel of the pistol into his neck. Brutus patted down Silas. He found nothing and stepped away.

"I'm like you, Brutus. We're killers. Thinkers. We're looking to preserve ourselves no matter the cost to others. We're the same. Can't you see that?"

"You better have something good."

Silas studied his fingers. "This facility, as I am sure you already realise, is not fully operational. The Athena Protocol was enacted far quicker than many in The Owls believed would happen. It caught this facility off guard. Orders were to have the supplies brought in. There has been an almost constant stream of supply wagons arriving and departing, but with the Carrion Virus taking hold in the city the deliveries stopped. Stopped suddenly. I've not checked the inventories as it wasn't my place to do so, but I believe from what I overheard that it is less than forty percent stocked."

"Stocked of what?"

"Food. Medical supplies. Clothing. Weapons. Essential mechanical parts. Fuel. Everything that should make this facility able to withstand years of siege by those infected with the virus."

"None of what you've told me is of value, Silas."

"It's not just the lack of supplies that will become an issue for you. The people who are to be living and working here are on their way. The last radio contact we made with the convoy placed them just outside the city limits. This facility may have seemed like a glittering prize, Brutus, but appearances can be deceiving."

"How many?"

"The convoy will consist of civilians important to The Owls of Athena. Top tier leadership and also the bulk of this facility's fighting power, the strike teams responsible for operations outside of the building. They'll be coming in heavy and hard."

"They don't know what's gone on here, right?"

"They fly drones over the area regularly. Each facility is in contact with the other. They'll know something is wrong due to the pause in contact."

"That's inevitable."

Silas knew a lot more, of that Brutus was certain. If he could keep him talking, he may become an asset. They were yet to secure the facility, and someone with inside knowledge, someone who would cooperate, would be of benefit. The rest of his team would not like it. But like all problems, Silas Salt could be dealt with at a later date.

CHAPTER 7

ALL THE WORLD WILL BE YOUR ENEMY

Daybreak brought little comfort to Gemma Findley. The uncomfortable evening spent cowering in the tiny shop brought aches and pains and hunger. She ripped open packets of cereal bars and chocolate biscuits. It was not her usual choice of breakfast, but there was little else on offer, and she hoped the sugar rush would bring some measure of warmth to her bones. She washed it all down with bottled water. It did little to appease her stomach.

She found her way to the small bathroom, did the necessities, washed her hands and splashed the freezing water that trickled from the tap onto her face. It caught her breath. She looked into the small mirror that hung on the wall.

"What are you going to do now, Gemma?"

Gemma headed back into the shop and hugged the electric heater.

The town was quiet. No cars, no faces. She could stay in the shop, wait for someone to happen by. It might never happen judging by how infrequent the roads were being travelled. Not just that, there was no guarantee whoever she met would be of help, or be infection free. She considered trying to find a car in one of the garages and driving out. Where to, she wasn't quite sure. What if she ran out of fuel in the middle of nowhere? She would freeze to death overnight. Or she could run into a group of infected. At least here she was safe and sheltered if only for the moment. The houses could hold useful items. She needed to check them first before deciding on a plan. Leave or stay, she needed to be as prepared as possible.

Outside, the wind whipped up throwing powdery snow into her face. She clung onto her backpack and pulled the lapels of her coat high. The few houses in the hamlet appeared much the same as they did the night before. Being alone never bothered Gemma a great deal. Before the outbreak she spent most evenings on her own. She wondered how many of her friends were still alive. It had been so long since she spared anyone a thought. Most were dead now, or perhaps shambling around the streets, one of the numberless infected.

No lights were visible in the first house, and the curtains were all drawn. Gemma traced a finger around the doorbell. She flipped the letter box open to look for signs of life. The hallway beyond was dark and quiet. Nothing moved in the house. She thought about calling through the letterbox but if there were infected she needed to avoid riling them. Stealth was paramount. The knife in her boot gave her a small measure of comfort. She waited a little longer, counting seconds in her head.

Still nothing. No noise other than the wind. Gemma moved around the house and through a flimsy side gate into the rear garden. Two footballs and a small set of goals protruded from the snow, the thin metal frame buckled and the net missing. Just behind them also poking out of the snow was a small, stone statuette, Hellenistic in design, a robed female with one breast revealed.

Large patio doors lead to a dining room. The sliding doors were both locked, not budging despite Gemma's best attempts to pull them free. The rear door was also secured.

Gemma pulled the partially naked statuette from the snow, struggled at first with the weight, then she launched it through the glass. The whole pane shattered.

Gemma stepped inside and headed to the kitchen. The room could have been occupied by humans not minutes before. Dirty cups and plates sat on the bench. Clothes were draped over hangers to dry. But the cupboards were close to empty. All that remained were packets of stir-in sauces, lentils and peas, and bread so mouldy it looked like an oversize dirty sponge. The light in the fridge was not working, and on the top shelf sat butter and two shrivelling peppers.

On the counter, next to the kettle and microwave, a number of letters were arranged each overlapping the last. Each envelope had a name printed in large block capitals. The first was addressed to

Aaron McGuiness. No address, no stamp. Whoever Aaron McGuiness was, she doubted he was going to return to inspect his mail. She ripped the envelope open.

Dear Aaron. If you're reading this we've gone. It's no longer safe here. We've lost power so often over the last few days we're not willing to risk being stuck. The TV for the most part is not broadcasting. The radio still works and we've been listing to updates. I've tried so hard to call you and your brother. Emails too. Nothing works. I hope and pray that you're both safe. Your dad is running low on medication. He's okay for the moment but things will become difficult if we can't find more.

We've decided to leave. The army has been broadcasting the last few hours. They've set up a camp not too far from here. They're calling all survivors to them. Your father agrees that we should go. They say they have medicine and can provide safety, food and shelter. We've no other option. We're leaving tonight. Your father has taken one of his maps and marked the position of the camp. If you read this, find us.

I know you wanted to stay and volunteer in the displacement centres but we need you. I need my boys with me and now more than ever. Help the people you meet. Always be kind. But come back to us, Aaron. You and your brother. Come back to us.

With all our love,
Mum and Dad x

Gemma studied the map. A thick marker had circled the exact location of the army camp. She traced a finger down the main arterial road that linked Aberdeen with Dundee. If she had a car, then she could navigate her way there. The camp itself seemed to be quite a distance to the West of the A90 road, beside a long snaking body of water. The nearby location names were not familiar, and travelling alone would be dangerous. But the army camp would perhaps offer her the only chance.

Gemma moved to the window and looked out to the garage.

***

Jane dimmed the lights and turned the car into the driveway of Carter's former employer. The children and Jacqui slept soundlessly. Carter bled from his arms. They had been forced to stop many times, the roads blocked by debris and wreckage, and Carter moved quickly to clear the way. Jane had applied makeshift bandages, all to the tune of Carter's protests, but the blood had seeped through.

The location of the home was exactly what Carter promised. Isolated. It was a grand house undergoing renovations. Parts of the roof were still to be installed. Sheets of blue canvass covered the holes. But a healthy billow of smoke rose from a chimney stack.

"You see that smoke?" asked Jane.

"I see it," said Carter, grimly.

"What should we do?"

"It's not our problem if someone is in there. It'll be their problem."

Carter pulled his handgun free from the holster and passed it to Jane. She accepted the heavy weapon with both hands.

"Stay here and keep an eye on Jacqui and the kids. I'm going in to investigate."

"What if you don't come back?" The words were out of her mouth before she could regret them.

"I'll be back, Jane. Keep your eyes open and don't be afraid to use that if you need to. Assume anyone out here is not friendly."

Carter opened the door quietly and stepped out. He readied his AR-15, slipping the sling into place. A light drizzle caused the evening sky to be a light shade of black. Carter moved like the consummate soldier he was, weapon up and scanning for threats. His movement was slightly hampered by a limp Jane had not previously noticed.

Jane unbuckled her seatbelt. There was a tightness in her chest, a clench that had visited her the first time she ran down an infected. It was yet to leave. Carter reached the door and pulled keys to the house from his vest pouch. He unlocked the door and disappeared.

"Where has Carter gone?" asked Jacqui, her voice sudden and low.

"We've arrived at the house. Carter's gone inside to make sure it's safe."

"There's smoke coming out of the chimney."

"I know," said Jane.

"I wish Eric was here."

"Carter is doing his best."

"What we saw on our way here. The people, those things. I could never have believed it all had gotten this bad. Eric never talked about what happened in Aberdeen really. But I knew it was bad. I could see it in his eyes. He wanted to tell me but didn't. And I'm glad he didn't."

"I don't talk about it either, Jacqui. I guess when you've gone through something like that the last thing you want to do is talk about it." Jane let out a sigh. "Maybe I'll check outside. Carter told me to keep a look out."

Jacqui stroked Luke's hair.

Jane slipped the Glock into the pocket of her coat. The rain was cold, but brought a peculiar calm. The tightness at her chest disappeared. She touched her pocket.

The property was protected by a thin screen of evergreen trees. There was only one road to the house and it snaked through the cover of trees, their high branches reaching across and touching. She looked back to the car. Luke's face was pressed to the window.

On the journey to the house, something bothered Jane. Many of the cars they passed contained the dead. Windows broken from the inside suggested an infected in the car killed the other occupants then made their escape. Carter had commented on it, too, and figured that families refused to follow the government's advice to make authorities aware of those who fell ill. No one wanted those they loved locked up in isolation. No one wanted those they loved executed. What would she do if it was someone she loved? But Jane had witnessed the progress of the virus. Those infected were no longer the people they once were. Those infected were no longer people.

"Jane."

She jumped. Carter stood at the door, his weapon in hand.

"What did you find?"

He walked down the steps. "There's people living in there. A family of three. I've secured them for now."

"Who are they?"

"I didn't stop to ask. A man, a woman and their teenage son. They didn't put up much resistance."

"You didn't hurt them, did you?"

"It's not a time for being tender, Jane. Get Jacqui and the kids. We'll decide what to do when inside."

Jacqui reached into the car and unbuckled her daughter, removing her gently. Katie was asleep in her mother's arms. Jane reached in and helped Luke out. She lifted him up and urged him to silence. Carter led them down a wide hallway, bare and lacking decoration. The walls were freshly painted, a bland shade of eggshell. The vague scent of paint hung in the air. A long sideboard with a plastic covering was on the left. Lights hung low down the centre of the hallway. Their footfall on the floorboards echoed. They reached two doors.

"Head in there. It's a bedroom," Carter said, opening the smaller door. "The other door leads to the living room. You stay with the kids, Jacqui. You come with me, Jane. The sooner we get this over with, the better."

Carter grabbed Jane by the wrist with unnecessary vigour.

***

Eric followed long and twisting roads which were little more than tracks cutting through snow choked farms. It seemed no vehicles had traversed that way for a time, and progress was slow. He occasionally caught sight of a lone figure on foot battling through the drifts but none made any attempt to move closer to Eric. Everyone was suspect of everyone. No one dared ask or help. The road eventually opened up, and the vehicle gained some speed.

Some miles on smouldering ruins of vehicles blocked the entire dual carriageway. Eric brought the Land Rover to a halt. He opened the door and put a foot out. Skye looked up from her sleep. He needed to see if there was a viable route through the destruction. If the road was clear, he would never have stopped.

Eric patted Skye. "You stay here and look after the car."

He pulled his weapon around. Years in the field told him he was looking at the result of an airstrike, a sustained bombardment. Over fifty cars ruined. Eric did not need to examine the wrecks closely to know there were charred bodies inside. Off to the left a bus lay on its side down a verge. The concussion of the blasts must have thrown it from the road. All the windows were shattered.

Eric's ankles dug into the wet earth. The seats of the bus had been ripped from the floor, and bodies lay covered in shattered glass. Those bodies wore the same blue ski jackets and furry boots worn by the infected that attacked the Ingram's farm, and the infected he saw not far from the farm. It may have been coincidence, or perhaps some were thrown clear, became infected and made their way toward the farm. Why did they wander in that direction? Why not elsewhere? They could have marched for days and never come into contact with another living soul. Was it just stupid chance that brought them to the Ingram's home?

Eric returned to the road. Skye's front paws were up on the dashboard and her tail wagged furiously. A flickering light far off to his left caught his eye. Did he miss something in his short reconnaissance?

"If there's anyone down there," he called, "you better come up now." Nothing moved. "Last chance."

Still nothing.

Eric moved forward, his feet wide ready to react to a threat. Two hundred metres away from his car, a flashlight pulsed weakly on a grassy mound. At the base of the mound and half-submerged in a pool of muddy rainwater lay a man, his face covered with a thick scarf. His skin was pale with the pallor of death, but unblemished, no signs of the virus. Two puncture wounds were positioned in his chest, markings consistent with a high-powered weapon. Did he run away from the fires? Was he gunned down? Where military troops nearby? Did they assume the man to be infected?

Eric hurried back to the Land Rover. He jumped in, and Skye tried to lick his face.

"Back in your seat, Skye."

She obeyed.

"You hungry?"

The dog's ears flew up.

"Me too."

Securing supplies would be his next priority. There was no break in the concrete barrier separating the north and south roads. He would have to double back until he found one.

***

Brutus headed into the courtyard, back out into the rain. Freddo stood under the shelter of the doorway, smoking a stubby cigar. He blew smoke into the gloomy morning, his eyes on Taylor and the minibus.

"We've got a problem," said Brutus.

"Just one?" Freddo flicked cigar ash to the ground.

"We're keeping Silas Salt."

Freddo shrugged as if expecting that course of action.

"A convoy's battling its way through the city. They're a few hours away at best."

"It was a matter of time before we'd be tangling with them." Freddo pointed to the minibus. "We need to get them out of here. Now."

"We need to break the news they'll be sent off without weapons."

"Your guess at the response?"

"It won't be a square dance with balloons."

The two men nodded a greeting to Taylor at the minibus.

"Alright!" shouted Brutus into the minibus. "I know certain promises were made however the situation has altered. You're

116

leaving in this fine vehicle, but not with an escort, and not with weapons."

"You know what you're sending us out to?"

"That's bullshit!"

"What? You're kidding right?"

"Shouldn't have trusted you!"

"Where's Silas?"

Brutus raised his AK-47. Behind, Freddo's weapon clicked to ready, Taylor's, too. Brutus considered shooting them all down where they sat. It would eliminate the chance of them linking up with The Owls of Athena units. But he would save the ammunition. Unarmed and in a lumbering vehicle, they would not last long.

"One of you get into the driver's seat and get the hell out of here," he ordered.

One man climbed behind the wheel. "You know you're all dead men, right? All of you. You don't know who you're screwing with!"

The door closed and the minibus pulled away.

"Get back to Roy, Taylor. Bring him and the families in, and fast. Get rid of the bodies inside, Freddo. Put them in the river."

Brutus crossed to where Magnus watched over the men captured in the yard. They were still bound and huddled in fear. He waved Magnus over, and whispered, "Set them loose, and walk them out the front door. Tell them they're free to go."

"They won't last long out there, Brutus. None of them are fighters. Just workers in the wrong place at the wrong time."

"I know. Once that's done, help Freddo with the bodies at the gate." Brutus returned inside to where Ash Gibbons watched over the managers and Silas. "Where's a cell for these three?"

"There are cells beneath the building, next to the supply vault," Silas answered.

"You have access?"

Silas nodded. "Of course."

"Get your ass moving." Brutus shoved Silas in the back.

Ash pulled the three managers to their feet, covering them with his handgun, and herded them like sheep.

***

Beneath the surface the long corridors were icy cold and not great in height. Brutus ducked his head more than once.

"How many levels are there beneath the surface?" asked Brutus.

"Several. I've never had cause to come down lower than this level but I know it goes deeper. I've heard them talking about *down below*."

The six cells were tucked away in a corner, the doors a dulled metal with no glass. Silas pushed aside the door when the lock disengaged.

"Where did you get that keycard from? Seems like it opens everything in this place."

"I took it from one of the managers. It's a handy thing to have."

The cell was nothing more than a large holding room, with a few benches, a toilet and a sink. There was no comfort in the room, no heating. The scantily clad managers would spend an uncomfortable time down there. All the better, thought Brutus. They might grow to be more compliant.

"Take off their blindfolds."

Silas did as was ordered. Brutus pulled a combat knife from his vest. He cupped the female's face. She tried to pull away but it only caused Brutus to tighten his hold.

"I'm going to cut your hands free. You're responsible for these other two. They need to shit or piss, you help them, understand?"

She nodded.

Brutus turned her around none too gently, and cut the restraints. Pressure marks marred her wrists. She rubbed at them. Brutus circled her like a shark waiting to feast. He put his knife to her face.

"I want you to think about your situation while I'm gone. I want you to remember how I look, how I smell. I want you to know that I hold your life in my hand." Brutus stroked her face. "I could leave you three down here, rotting and starving. Or I could make your death so painful you'll be praying for the end. Think about your situation. I don't know your name. I don't need to know your name. To me, you're nothing but a corpse waiting to fall. Understand I'm the worst person you could meet. And I will be back. Lock them in."

Silas swiped his keycard at the scanner. A soft buzzer sounded and the lock engaged.

"Key," said Brutus, his hand outstretched.

Silas passed it over with only a momentary hesitation.

"Take me to the storage vault."

They walked along the corridors.

"How is the power being supplied?" Brutus's voice seemed to boom in the still of the confined space.

"At the moment the power is being run from the grid. I believe they assumed one day after everything went to shit the power would fail, so there are generators in the plant room. Clean power is supplied in a limited way through solar panelling and a few other means I'm not sure about. The building is designed to power down during certain hours. Only essential systems are left running."

"So if the power from the grid went down the generators would kick in?" asked Ash.

"It's something the facility managers would be able to answer. I had no cause to know about things like that."

"You know much about some, Silas, yet little about more. Are you being choosey?"

Silas shrugged. "This is the vault. You'll have to do the honours as I seem to be without my keycard."

Silas was knocked aside by an impatient Brutus. He stumbled dramatically but made no verbal protest. Brutus unlocked the door, and it opened inward, hissing pistons taking the strain. The opening was large enough for two men to enter abreast. Brutus pulled Silas in with him, Ash followed, his hand resting on his Glock.

The storage vault was like an aircraft hangar. The curved roof boasted long tubular lights which powered up with the doors opening. They flickered to life bathing the vault in clinical light. Row upon row of storage cages, like a distribution warehouse, lined the sides, each labelled clearly. *Clothing-Male-Adult. Clothing-Female-Adult. Male Footwear. Female Footwear. Outdoor equipment. Batteries.* Off to the right sat large industrial cooling and freezing rooms for fresh food and meats. A narrow service elevator disappeared upward, most likely a direct line to the kitchens. Stocks were low.

Brutus made a beeline for the ammunition store to the rear of the vault. It a sturdy cage, the door unlocked. Boxes of ammunition were piled in containers, but the weapon racks were only partially stocked.

"Where are the guns?" he asked stepping into the lockup.

"I told you before, we're forty percent stocked at best. I guess most of the weapons just never made it. There's three fifty-calibre machine guns that need to be installed on the walls. Each has around two-thousand rounds. I regret to say what you see is what you get."

Food. Clothes. Even medicines were things that Brutus could procure from the city if needed. Weapons and ammunition were not. Three heavy machine guns, a collection of assault rifles and a handful of grenades was not the arsenal that he hoped for.

"Get back to the surface," Brutus said to Ash, "and get the fifty's installed. I want the gate closed and reinforced as soon as we can. Take him with you."

Brutus sat down next to the ammunition stacks and pulled his empty magazines free from his tac vest. He laid them out neatly, then selected the right ammunition and reloaded each magazine in turn. There, alone in the vault, the clicking of the ammo slipping in sounded as loud as an actual gunshot.

***

No vehicles were parked in driveways or garages. Some pantries offered a small selection of canned tuna and corned beef. Gemma found clean a pair of clean jeans, a warm jumper that was much too large for her and two pairs of underwear and socks. She rummaged through a sideboard in the hallway and pulled out a small radio and flashlight.

Sometime in the early morning the power went out, prompting her to make a move. She found a black mountain bike in a garage. It looked close to new, the chain clean, the sprockets shiny. She found a small spanner and lowered the seat. In happier times the prospect of a bike ride was relished. Now it was going to be hard work. She hoped clear tracks would be out there somewhere, because those wide tyres wouldn't get too far in thick snow.

**

Jane shrugged off Carter's grasp and speared him with a look of defiance. He'd hurt her arm and she rubbed at it. What was going through his head?

The living room was wide and airy. Logs snapped and popped in a grand fireplace. The mantelpiece was ornate and she guessed cost a pretty penny. The curtains were drawn. A man, woman and teenage boy lay on their stomachs on the floor, their hands secured behind their back with plastic ties.

"Please don't hurt us," pleaded the man into the floor. "If you let us go, we'll never come back. You have my word. We didn't mean any harm."

Carter remained silent, his arms folded and resting against the stock of his weapon. Jane took this to mean she was to take the lead.

"Who are you?" she asked, her voice shaky.

"My name is Harold Crossly. My wife Isabelle and my son Elliot." Blood had dried at a cut on his temple.

"Tell me what happened, how you came to be here."

Harold Crossly tried to look up from the floor, but could only cough. "We left our home two days ago. The advice was we should stay put but things were going from bad to worse. Looters and those things. We packed up the car and found ourselves stuck with thousands of others clogging the motorway. Nobody could move. Then helicopters flew overhead and opened fire. We grabbed what we could from the car and walked for two days. Then we stumbled across this place. It's not our way to walk into another's home, but we were desperate. That's the truth."

"How long have you been here?"

"Two days. We were going to move on, but—"

"We wouldn't make it far in this weather," said the wife, Isabelle.

"You're trespassing," said Carter.

"We'll leave," said Harold, apologetically.

"We can't leave," Isabelle argued. "I can't walk further. I just can't." She wept quietly.

"We have to." Harold spoke not with anger, but as someone resigned to their fate, no matter the outcome.

Jane bent down to the floor and looked into Isabelle's face. The woman stopped crying and blinked over and again.

"Carter, cut them free."

"No."

Jane stood. "They're no threat, surely you can see that."

"Too risky."

"Too risky? They're victims here, too."

"My job is to protect you."

"They need our help, Carter."

"If we start helping everyone we come across, we're going to get it wrong."

An ember launched from the fireplace.

"We're not going to turn them away. Not like this."

"What's happening?" Jacqui walked in, and stood close to Carter.

"You tell her," said Carter.

"He wants to keep this family tied up on the floor."

"I'm only doing what Eric asked. To keep you all safe."

"Is it necessary?" asked Jacqui.

Both Carter and Jane answered at the same time.

"No!"

"Yes!"

Jacqui gifted Carter a questioning look, and in that moment Jane knew Jacqui believed as she did.

Carter pulled the combat knife from the sheath on his belt. He handed the weapon to Jane. "You're responsible for them. Understand? I'm going to walk the perimeter."

Carter stormed from the living room.

"I'm sorry about this," said Jane crossing to Harold first. "Times like these tend to make people wary." She still had the Glock in her coat pocket. If she got this wrong, and the family were a danger it would be up to her to intervene.

Jane cut the cords and helped Harold to sit upright. "That's a nasty cut you have to your temple."

"I don't think your friend was taking any chances," he said, helping his wife to her feet. "Let's get you onto the sofa, Isabelle."

Elliot sat on the floor rubbing his wrists and staring into the fire. He made no eye contact with anyone.

"They were fleeing their home but became stuck on the roads," Jane explained to Jacqui. "There was a helicopter attack and they fled here by chance."

"I'm Jacqui Mann. This is Jane and Carter is our ... protector."

"This is your home?"

"It's our friend's home," lied Jacqui. "Maybe we can find something to make tea in?"

"Elliot? Come here and thank the ladies for their kindness."

Their son did as he was told, and wiped at his face. No one acknowledged his tears.

"Let me have a look at your cut," she said to Harold. "I'm a nurse."

Isabelle smiled thinly. "Thank you for your help. We're all very grateful."

Harold nodded saying, "Times have changed. I don't recognise the country we live in anymore."

Times had changed irrevocably, or so it seemed.

"I'll check on the kids," said Jacqui.

"Oh," said Isabelle. "You have children here?"

"Two. Excuse me."

Isabelle placed her hand on Harold's knee as Jane examined the cut.

"So, Elliot, how old are you?"

The fire burned on.

***

The village was small, less than fifty semi-detached dwellings clustered along the road. The sign which should have announced the name of the village was missing, perhaps toppled by a wayward vehicle and now buried under snow.

The radio repeated the same broadcasts and news flashes over and again. He turned it off. Skye panted next to Eric, looking longingly between him and outside. She had not drank or answered the call of nature in a good few hours.

"Soon," he said, patting her.

Eric brought the vehicle to a halt. He wound down the window letting the cold air inside. Skye sniffed, her head directed to the fresh flow of air. Making sure nothing was lurking nearby, Eric switched the engine off. A quiet broken only by the wind overtook them. Eric watched the calm of the village. A few pinpricks of light in the windows broke the otherwise drab exterior. It was the type of place he would have driven through previously, barely registering it as a location. Nothing seemed to move amount the silent houses. Nothing that would indicate danger. He switched the engine back on and moved toward the village.

Only one house in the village had a driveway that was open and unobstructed. Eric pulled left, reversing into it. Being off the road seemed like a sensible option. He opened the door and jumped out, and clicked his fingers to Skye. The dog jumped out in one bound, sniffed at the air, and then the ground and squatted for a long time. Eric clicked his fingers again, and ordered Skye back into the Land Rover. He wanted to check the place out further before he allowed the dog to roam free.

Smoke hung heavily in the air. He brought his rifle ready. The house he selected to park in looked abandoned, the front door was open, no car in the drive and no lights on. Signage *Beware of Dog* was attached to the fence.

Eric pushed the door open with his foot. Inside was a cluttered hallway. Discarded clothes were flung about the floor. Full plastic bottles of water were collected at the foot of the stairs. Shopping bags, stuffed with items were collected by the doorway. Something moved upstairs, like someone walking back and forth incessantly. He thought about calling out, announcing his intentions. Whoever was there must have been unaware of his presence. Perhaps the Land Rover had been quieter than he thought.

The stairs were carpeted. His tread would be silent. But the first step creaked under his weight. He froze. No more movement came. He took the next step, sure to place his feet to the edges. And then the next. No creaking. One step at a time, his eyes and firearm up. Twelve steps in total and he reached the landing. A noise came from the room directly in front of him.

"You don't want to go in there."

Eric spun left, rifle aimed. A man sat on the floor at the far end of the hallway, propped up, his back to the wall. Blood seeped from wounds to his arms and chest.

"I won't hurt you," he said, laboured.

"What's in there?"

"One of them. It's wounded. I couldn't finish it off before it got me."

"What's your name?"

"It doesn't matter. I'm nobody now. I'm someone who didn't listen when everyone else told me to leave. I don't suppose you've got a cigarette?"

"That stuff'll kill you."

The man chuckled. It was a hollow sound. "Are you a soldier?"

"No. I'm just looking for a few things then I'll be on my way."

The man spat froth.

"Take what you want. It's not like I'll be needing it." He wiped his chin. "I can feel it you know? It's like a burning beneath my skin. If I close my eyes I know I won't open them again. The one that got me was my neighbour. Broke through my door, came up the stairs. I put a knife in its head, but not before it did this."

He held up his arm. Three bite marks, one opened a large gash. "You heading to the army camp?"

"What camp?"

"You haven't heard of it? Well, I need a favour first, then I'll give you directions."

Eric didn't move.

"It's not a difficult one. I don't want to turn into one of those things. You can make it so I don't wake up."

"Okay," Eric responded after a time.

"My name is Foggie. That's what my friends call me. You want to know why they call me that?"

"Sure."

"I grew up in a town way up north from here. You'll never have heard of it. Aberchider but the locals call it Foggie." He winced in pain. "Doesn't seem that important now, does it? What was I saying? Yeah, the camp. Keep following this road and head west, always west. In fifteen miles or so you'll come to a hill with trees at the summit. The camp's up there. You'll find signs to get you in." He grimaced again. "Take what you need. There's food in the kitchen cupboards. The freezer is pretty full of stuff. In the hallway there's water bottled up. It's fresh. My clothes, too. You look about my size. They might do you well out there. In the bathroom, you'll find a small leather bag. Inside I've put all the medicine I could scrape together, over the counter supplies and some antibiotics. There's first aid things, too. The food should last you a week or two if you go easy. Jesus, it's hurting."

Foggy dipped his head, his chin resting on his chest. "Good luck to you."

Eric pulled the trigger.

Noises came louder from the room ahead. Eric couldn't suffer the infected contained in the room to live while he gathered supplies. He needed to make the house safe. Eric moved to the door. Blood from Foggy or the infected stained the handle and key than dangled from the lock. Eric planted a sturdy kick to the door, smashing it open, swinging inward. He stepped in, rifle raised covering the angles. The infected lay on the floor of the bedroom, one hand gripping the leg of a small table near the corner. It was naked, a large kitchen knife protruding from its skull. It tried to rise to reach Eric but could not. It slumped back and shuddered. Eric put a single shot in its head. It stopped moving.

Eric retrieved Skye from the car, and closed the front door behind them. He pulled two glass bowls from the kitchen cupboard, filled them with water and placed them on the floor. Skye drank and drank, much of the water flicking onto the floor.

"Thirsty, girl?"

Cans of dog food sat at the back of one of the shelves in the pantry. Eric pulled one out, stabbed at the lid with his knife and tore open the top. He didn't bother finding another bowl, and simply tipped the contents onto the floor. Skye sniffed before wolfing it all down. Her eyes darted to Eric twice, and each time her tail wagged.

"And hungry, too?"

The army camp provided the best option. If he could make it there then there was a chance his return to his family could be facilitated. If there were other elements of the armed forces still fighting then they would be making supply runs between each operating base. By road and air. Maybe even sea. Eric could barter his way. In times like this, an experienced operator like him would be worth making special arrangements for. It sparked a glimmer of hope. He threw down three glasses of the cold water from the tap. Skye crept up and rubbed her face into his leg. Eric sank down to the floor, letting the dog curl up next to him. A few hours rest first and then he'd gather supplies. Fifteen miles. Only fifteen.

CHAPTER 8

I'LL FIGHT TILL FROM MY BONES MY FLESH BE HACKED

Brutus ran from the underground chambers, a holdall over his shoulder. The rain fell with more insistence, and his boots scattered water from the quickly growing puddles.

"Over here." Ash Gibbons waved from the doorway to the reception area.

Brutus altered course, and took shelter in the doorway. Silas Salt stood silent yet focused off to the right of Ash.

"They're coming?" he asked, setting his heavy burden down.

"Roy's up there." He pointed to the roof. "He's relocated to the helipad and spotted the convoy moving through the city."

"How much time do we have?"

"Half an hour. Maybe."

Ash did not seem overly concerned by the revelation, too long a soldier to show outward panic. But there was a feeling in the air. Though nobody looked at him now, he felt their eyes and expectations keenly.

The gate to the facility was closed, a steel barrier, reinforced with strong beams with rolls of razor wire on top. On either side of the gate sat machine gun posts under camo nets and squat canopies. Freddo manned the gun to the left, Taylor to the right. Niall stood by the gate, making sure it was barred fast. He rattled the mechanism until satisfied, and gave Brutus the thumbs up.

Magnus came down the stairs behind, carrying an armful of MP5s. He laid them on the counter. "Thought we might need these. I'll get the rest and the ammo." He disappeared back up the stairs at a run.

"Are your families inside?"

"Murray and Taylor brought them in. They're on the fifth floor, facing out onto the river."

"Good." Any indirect fire would be less likely to put them in danger located there.

The rain was doing a fantastic job of washing away the blood at the door.

"I want everyone issued with an MP5 and as much ammo as they can carry. I don't want anyone running dry."

"Give me a weapon, Brutus," said Silas. "I'm very handy in a tight spot, you know that."

"I want Silas secured to the strut over there."

"You're making a mistake, Brutus. I could make the difference here between you keeping control of this place or you all dying. Do you really want to take that chance?"

"Tie him tight, and make sure he doesn't have any hidden blades on him. Legs, too." To Silas, Brutus said, "Not another word, understand?"

Ash pulled Silas to the metal strut, pointed his Glock at his head and pushed him down, then secured his arms behind his back around the structure using plastic ties.

Magnus returned, Roy by his side, and they dumped more weapons on the reception counter.

"Brutus." Roy flicked his head. "A word." He moved toward the stairs, away from ears, and Brutus followed.

"You've left your watch. Better be important."

"Magnus mentioned the name Silas. You know who he is?"

"Nothing more than the name."

"Green Zone in Baghdad. There was one guy who went off base and raped and killed a young family."

"I remember. He returned covered in their blood. Silas wasn't the name though, was it?"

"No. Wayne Salt. I heard he'd been taken away for prosecution. Heard nothing since."

Brutus pulled at his beard. "Not a word to anyone else on the team for now, okay?"

"We should kill him, now."

"Yes, we should. But we might need his knowledge to get us through this shit. Tell me about the convoy heading here."

They moved back to the reception area. Brutus picked up magazines for the MP5s and stuffed them into his pockets.

"Seven vehicles in all. Two medium sized single-decked buses. They're battling their way here, so should be a little gun-weary when they arrive. How're we going to play this?"

"When they pull up to the gate we open up with the fifty-calibres. Anyone who makes it out we'll engage with small arms from the walls. If we're lucky, we'll take them all out before they have a chance to form any resistance. If not, we need to put up such a front that they scatter and think twice before coming back."

"The Owls are going to come after us. Maybe not next week but some time."

"Maybe," said Brutus, handing three magazines to Roy. "Or maybe they'll have their hands full with the mess they've created. There's a whole world of infected out there, and the infected don't look at The Owls as off limits. So, if The Owls come for us it won't be soon. There's a whole city out there to fight before they get close to us. I can guarantee that." Brutus endured Roy's gaze.

"Good luck, then."

"To us all," said Brutus, smiling.

Roy snapped a magazine into the MP5 and dashed back toward the stairwell. It was a long climb back to the top of the building and the protruding helipad. He made it to the top without incident. No hidden surprises.

"Magnus, see that everyone has some of these magazines. Take the bag, and dish 'em out."

Brutus crossed to Silas. "I'm leaving you now, Silas. You be a good boy while we're away. Free yourself from your restraints or cause me any inconvenience, no matter how small, I will make sure you suffer in a way only a few people in this world could ever believe."

"So many threats, Brutus? When all I've tried to do is help you."

Brutus threw a pointed kick into Silas's ribs.

Ash was at his side. "We can deal with this piece of shit after. Come on."

Brutus sidestepped Ash enough to look directly down at Silas. "Think on it, Wayne."

Silas's face twitched.

"You say you know me? Then you know I am a man of my word. Do anything to jeopardise us here and you'll see exactly what it means when I keep a promise."

Brutus marched out into the courtyard. Magnus was on the walls, distributing the ammo. Niall walked over to Brutus, both men were quickly soaked by the rain.

Niall wiped wet hair from his face. "We're as ready as we'll ever be." He looked back up to the walls. "I wish we had more bodies to cover all the ground. It's a lot of wall."

"They're coming from one direction. And I doubt any of them have brought a ladder. You're with me, right?"

"Of course. To the ends of the earth, it would seem," he said with a smirk.

Together they climbed the narrow stairs, up to the wall. From the outside the walls underwhelmed Brutus some. Now, standing atop them, they felt imposing and strong. Wave after wave of infected could rush the walls for naught. They were so close to winning. He could feel it. One battle, then a respite to take stock.

The parapet was high enough that if Brutus was to kneel down, he would be concealed from view. Plenty of cover. Brutus ducked into the machine gun nest below the camouflage canvass. The rain drummed out a noisy cacophony. Taylor loaded the .50 calibre weapon, checking each box of ammunition was ready. Three men beneath the cover was a tight fit. Brutus squeezed his shoulder before leaving them and headed along the wall to the edge of the gate.

He waved to Freddo. "Alright?"

Freddo held up a thumb.

Niall tapped Brutus on the shoulder. He pulled an earpiece free, letting it dangle on the cord.

"I said no radios," snapped Brutus. "We don't know if they're listening."

"You want Roy running up and down all them stairs to report updates? They're coming. They'll be in view very soon."

Brutus swung a backhanded punch, striking Niall on the chin, sending him back a few steps.

"You might've just compromised this whole endeavour. I said no shitty radios for a reason."

"It doesn't matter now," said Niall, rubbing his chin. He spat. "They're coming. We're here. Let's deal with it then worry about whether I should have used the radio or not. Okay? Now, where do you want me?"

"Far corner, up on the wall, past Freddo. I'll be in other corner. Magnus will support Freddo and Ash will support Taylor. Roy will watch from above. Nobody fires until I give the word." He turned from Niall before the urge to punch him again was overwhelming.

The men moved into position. Brutus reached the end of the front-facing wall, where it joined with the barrier that ran to the riverside. He sank down and brought his weapon up. The MP5 sat awkwardly, so he removed the strap and placed the magazines neatly around him. He adjusted his AK-47 leaving it to hang. Now he just had to wait.

Niall whistled, two short and sharp sounds. He pointed up to where Roy was stationed.

Their visitors were coming. The long street leading to the building was deserted. Buildings lined both sides of the road, many boarded up or secured with shutters. Graffiti brightened the dull exterior. When the recession hit, businesses suffered and this was the legacy. Builds left with no further purpose.

The first vehicle came into view running ahead of the main convoy. A dark car, with an armed man standing up through the sunroof. A pickup with more armed men in the back followed. Then two small buses. Bringing up the rear, three more pickups with men clinging to the back. The last vehicle stopped and the men opened fire back the way they had come.

The lead car and first pickup pulled up to the gate. One man opened the passenger door and got out. "Open the goddamned gate," he shouted. "The whole city will be down on top of us soon. Hey! I can see you up there. Open the gate! Now!"

"The mechanism's jammed," replied Freddo. "We're working on it."

"Don't take too long. Those things are everywhere."

The men below formed a perimeter around the vehicles. Brutus counted nine. They were tightly packed, feet from the cars, and too close to the walls for the heavy weapons to reach. The walls provided cover to the nearest enemy. The firing arcs of the 50s would not reach them. Brutus signalled to Ash to be ready to hurl grenades down below. Ash gave the thumbs up and crawled back past the gun placement passing on the order.

The buses pulled up, their brakes whining the arrival. Tinted windows concealed the numbers inside. The final three vehicles pulled up and formed a makeshift barrier across the road. The security team alighted and took positions aiming their weapons back toward the city.

"Hey, assholes, open the gate. Hell's about to rain on us."

Brutus gave the signal. Ash Gibbons launched three grenades over the wall. More were thrown from the far side. Brutus fired three suppressed rounds, taking out the soldier that cursed at them. He fell back into the sodden street. The 50s opened up, barking out their lethality. Both gunners aimed for the buses. Roy was accurate from his position on the helipad. Heavy calibre shots tore through the thin carapace of the buses. The grenades exploded in a dull flash. Men cried out below. Brutus fired into the buses. The windscreens shattered and the driver slumped forward.

Brutus swapped his AK-47 for the MP5. He exposed himself and opened fire on the men blow. The initial blasts hit all the soldiers. One crawled away on elbows, his legs uselessly dragging behind. Brutus hosed him with fire. Reloading came at the same time. Survivors in the buses dashed for the cover of the buildings behind where the convoy stopped.

"Get the fifties firing!" screamed Brutus.

They fired again, first one, then the other. The rounds were sent at anything that moved. Smoke rose from engines and the buses became little more than bullet-ridden wrecks.

Some made it to two of the pickups that pulled out of formation and drove back toward the city. Shots hit the walls.

Brutus downed into cover. Taylor's 50 stopped firing and he, too, hid from the incoming shots. They waited for a lull in the engagement, the wall providing plenty cover to shelter the storm of bullets. Brutus waved Taylor back onto the heavy weapon. Taylor fired again, down into the street. The heavy rounds punched holes in the warehouses as if they were constructed of wood. The enemy retreated, moving back into the confines of the streets beyond.

Brutus raised his hand, an order to hold fire. "Everyone okay?"

The team checked in, one by one. Brutus kicked shell casings away from underfoot. They tumbled from the wall and down into the courtyard. The battle went well. Better than well. They managed to kill or reroute much of the military force sent to secure the building.

Niall climbed the stairs. "Roy's radioed down. A group of sixty to a hundred infected are on their way."

Brutus looked over the wall. Bodies lay over the road. More would be trapped inside the vehicles. A few were likely wounded and hoping to find an opportunity to crawl away and survive. He could not allow them to simply creep away. With the infected soon to be roaming outside, he considered letting the infected do it for them? They were too unreliable to trust. He would organise a sweep of the immediate area once they had time to pause, rearm and confirm their orders.

"We'll let this building do what it was designed for. Keep a watch for now, and stay in position. Don't fire unless you need to. I'll want a sweep outside the walls to take out anyone that survived all this."

In time Brutus could rely on the integrated surveillance systems that the building boasted, but not until the cameras were repaired. Once this was done, they could rely more on these systems rather than have people out on the walls day and night. The cameras were one of the many problems which required his attention.

From above, the faint but unmistakable sound of an aircraft engine thudded.

***

Surreal. That was the only way Ryan Bannister could describe his life in the sanctuary in the centre of London. Breakfast was served in a communal hall, something that looked like the dining room of an extremely expensive school. A buffet of dried fruits, yoghurt, ham, cheese, bread and cereal was offered in buffet form. Tea and coffee was served from urns on trestles to the side, with an array of sugars and milks and all kinds of substitutes.

The noisy business of eating the first meal in sanctuary was a curious thing. Some seemed strangely excited, others understandably wary, others chose to find seats away from chatty groups, preferring to keep eyes down and pick at their meal with cutlery rather than eat. Ryan should have made an effort to introduce himself to others, but he felt little like talking.

The constant ripple of gunfire outside was almost lost by the busy conversations.

Ryan shoved some ham and cheese into his mouth, chewed, swallowed, then tried the dried apricots and yoghurt. It was all delicious. Perhaps his time here was going to be more enjoyable than he anticipated.

"Ladies and gentlemen! Ladies and gentlemen, if I can have your attention, please?" A woman in a slim-fitting suit stood at the head of the eating hall, two guards standing to her side.

"We hope you've enjoyed your breakfast. From here we shall begin your induction. You will be given a tour of the facilities, instructions on procedures that are relevant, and you will be assigned tasks and chores."

A hand tapped him on the shoulder.

Law.

"Mr. Crispin would like to see you. Now."

"Now?" he said with his mouth full.

"Now."

"What about my induction?"

"He was very insistent."

Ryan wondered if Law ever took the stick out of his ass. He shoved a piece of toast into his mouth and stood, but stood too quickly and tipped his chair to the floor. It clattered at an unfortunate break in the briefing.

"Pardon me," he said, again his mouth full, and returned the chair to an upright position. He found himself bowing to the room twice as he backed his way out.

They reached the lift. Law swiped his card at the scanner, opening the doors.

"How are you finding it here in London?" asked Ryan, as the doors closed.

"Don't talk." Law pushed the button for the highest floor.

The lift rose up, the gentle hum of the mechanisms doing little to alleviate his sudden nervousness. The doors opened and Law lead him out of the lift and along a long corridor toward a set of double doors. Law knocked, opened one door and nodded crisply at Ryan to enter.

Hector Crispin sat straight-backed behind a wide desk. The curtains were drawn and the room was dark at the corners, the one desk lamp making Hector appear ghoulish.

"You wanted to see me, Mr. Crispin, Hector, sir?

"Take a seat, Ryan."

He did as ordered and sat into a leather chair at the desk. The light that illuminated Hector altered. The ghoul vanished. Hector's face was quite red, his nose bulbous.

"I wanted you here for a few reasons, the most important being an invaluable lesson, one I mean to impress upon you. Law, you may leave us now."

Law moved away silently. Hector pushed a button on a small speaker to his right, then fiddled with a speaker on his desk. Static crackled then disappeared.

"Ah, there we are," said Hector, leaning toward the speaker. "Captain Mathers, for the benefit of my new companion repeat what you can see right now."

The sound from the speaker was grainy, machinery in the background making it grittier.

"We've circled the building. The convoy was halted at the gate and came under attack from those inside the building. We've been depleted. I can see one sentry on the helipad."

"Captain, you have permission to proceed. We want our building back."

"Yes, sir."

Hector switched the speaker off.

"Not only were our people late in reaching the Glasgow facility, they have been prevented from taking up residence, Ryan, and with lethal consequences. I have many friends there and I do not know their fate. Whoever has done this will pay a dear price."

"And this Captain Mathers, he will attempt to wrestle control back, Mr. Crispin?"

"Indeed he will, Ryan. I wanted you here to witness the price of leadership. No matter how many plans or contingencies one has, things can and do go wrong. You need to be adaptable, change and move forward as best you can, and not surrender to panic."

Ryan nodded, listening but not understanding the point of the lesson.

"Do you know why I pulled you out of the induction today?"

"To speak to me?"

Hector's forehead creased.

"About something important?" Ryan added.

"By all rights, you should be down there and handed a menial chore. That would be payment for the protection that is being offered. So, do you know?"

Ryan shook his head. "I've got nothing other than that, sir."

"You perhaps are correct, Ryan. Yes, what I have to discuss with you is important, important to me. It's because you are all I have left of your father."

"My father was dear to you. I wish I had known him more."

"He was brilliant and I loved him dearly. I wish he were here now. Every day I wish it with all my being. This was his dream as much as mine. You are the shard of your father I can't help but cling to. You will be spared from the mundane tasks that await those below."

"Cool."

"Cool, Ryan?"

"I mean thank you."

"You are welcome. I will find something more productive for you, something less menial. We have all the time in the world to decide how to progress." Hector picked up a large coffee mug and sipped. His hand shook. "Let me tell you why I am keen to see the building in Glasgow taken back. Here and the sanctuary in Glasgow are part of a finely crafted network. We shall rely on each other for support in the times ahead. And, perhaps just as importantly, my daughter is there. I won't abandon her."

"Your daughter, Mr. Crispin, Hector, sir?"

***

A helicopter approached, coming in low. Brutus ran, leaping down the last steps of the stairs into the courtyard, and splashing through the puddles.

"Stay in post," he shouted. "Could be a counter attack."

Niall appeared at Brutus's side, running with him. He touched his earpiece. "I can't raise Roy."

The helicopter hovered above the helipad. A heavy machine gun opened up from the side. They pounded up the few steps and entered the building. Silas was gone.

"He's a dead man." Brutus pulled his Glock from the holster. "You see him before I do, you shoot him."

They reached the stairwell and took the steps three at a time. The higher they climbed, the louder the din of the helicopter's engines. Brutus breathed hard, grasped the banister to haul himself up that last steps. The top floor was a narrow corridor with two rooms on either side. At the far end, a metal hatch opened to the helipad, the double doors flung aside. They approached with weapons ready. The engines of the helicopter blotted out all other sounds.

Brutus climbed the three steps out of the building and onto the platform.

The helicopter's rotors continued to spin. Seven men lay dead or bleeding out on the helipad. Roy lay closest to them, face down, riddled with wounds to his back and legs.

Niall checked for a pulse. "He's gone," he yelled.

The rotors slowed and slowed some more until they stopped. Someone moved in the cockpit.

Silas Salt slipped out of the aircraft, and raised his hands in the air. Brutus rushed him.

"No, Brutus. I saved your little kingdom. But I was too late to save your friend."

Brutus had his hands around Silas's neck. "What are you talking about?"

Silas coughed. "I saved you." He coughed again.

"You did this?"

"Yes. I kept what was yours, kept it for you, and I've given you another mode of transport."

"How?"

"I heard the helicopter, cut my bonds and came up here. Your friend was already dead, killed before they landed. I simply approached with my hands up. I'm still in my uniform."

"I don't believe him." Niall kept his weapon ready. "He was searched. Nothing to cut the ties."

"I'm proficient in my trade."

"Why?" asked Brutus.

"Maybe I dislike how The Owls of Athena operate. Maybe I see a better chance of things working out here with you."

Brutus dragged Silas over the dead and to the edge of the pad. Brutus held him out over the edge. For the first time since meeting, Silas showed fear. He flailed his arms and let out a screech. The rain poured down.

"A friend of mine is lying dead behind me and all you can do is riddle me this and that? I told you if you moved from being tied up down there, you were a dead man."

"If I didn't, you'd all be dead. You need me more than ever, Brutus. You need more men. This attack has shown you that. I can help you. Please!"

Brutus would have loved to release his grip and watch the devil of a man splatter below. But he sensed Silas may have been right. He may need him. He pulled him up and flung him to the ground.

"Talk. And this better be good."

Silas crawled to his knees. "You're right, I could have let The Owls take this place back, but the truth is I've been planning to get out sooner rather than later. Some of my men are in the city. Guys I've worked with for years. They're fighters, like you and me. Tough men. I could bring them here. If we work together we can survive whatever the Carrion Virus and the infected throw at us. And I'm a pilot. I can fly that thing."

"You're going over the edge, Silas." Brutus picked the man up by his collar again, certain he should launch Silas over the precipice.

"Brutus! The woman you've got down in the cells, she's the daughter of one of The Owls, a very important Owl."

***

The more Jacqui and Jane talked with the Crosslys, the more Jane decided she'd made the correct decision. She liked having them around. Despite what they must have gone through, they presented as a normal family, loving and caring, conversant and interesting. Elliot avoided conversing with the adults, but chatted with Luke and Katie, and in turn the two siblings were overjoyed at the prospect of new company.

Jacqui managed to boil some water using an old pan and the large, open fire. Drinking hot tea and watching the family relax was a welcome change of pace. They sat on the sofa together, close. Speaking in hushed tones. But the weight of the weapon in her pocket reminded her to be on guard no matter what.

The door opened, Carter leaned in, cleared his throat. "Can I have a word?"

"Carter," said Jacqui, "I've made you some tea. Come in and join us."

"Maybe later," he said, still not entering the room. "Jane, a moment."

Jane followed Carter and pulled the door closed behind her. She kept her hands wrapped around the mug of tea. The hallway was a frozen tomb compared to the living room.

"I suppose they're staying," he said, arms folded over the stock of his weapon.

"They are. We couldn't just turn them away, Carter. We wouldn't have thrown people in need out a few months ago. We can't do it now. They need our help. They won't survive out there alone. What we've seen out there and in Aberdeen has at least prepared us for this in a small way. These people fled for their lives from something they don't understand. They'll die out there," she said again.

He shook his head. "Have you checked them thoroughly for the virus?"

"Just an initial check."

Carter's brow creased.

"Okay, I'll check them more thoroughly."

"You've got the fire burning too high. The smoke will be visible for miles?"

"So we'll dim the fire. We're doing the best we can, Carter. You too. Come inside for a bit, warm yourself up. You're soaked through."

"No. Give them a thorough inspection and twice. I'm going to sweep the perimeter again."

"Then I'll come with you."

"You need to be in there, watching them. I don't trust them. Eric wouldn't either." Carter walked away muttering to himself.

CHAPTER 9

DISPERSE

Eric rounded a corner and the engine spluttered and died. The fuel gauge had hovered in the red for half an hour, and he knew the inevitable.

"I hope you're ready for a walk, girl?"

Skye titled her head, listening.

Eric pulled on his coat and gloves, secured his weapons ready for quick use and stepped out of the Land Rover. Skye followed with a jump and a shake. The amount of supplies in the rear was more than one man could carry. Eric sifted through what was there, deciding what were essentials. He guessed they had ten miles to go before reaching the army camp. They needed to make it to the camp in one journey. To stop and camp in these conditions would be a death sentence.

Before packing the last into his backpack he took a swig of water from a bottle, removed a glove, cupped his hand and poured water for Skye. It was incredibly cold and his fingers threatened to lose all feeling. Skye drank hungrily, and Eric squeezed his fist over and again before returning it to the glove.

The backpack couldn't possibly hold more, and they left the safety of the Land Rover in search of the army camp. His strides sunk him knee-deep into the snowdrift. Skye trotted ahead, her legs sinking to her belly.

"I bet you wish you were back home, hey Skye?"

The dog turned for only a second.

"You had a cosy bed by the fire, and good food to eat. You know where I would like to be? Back home with Jacqui and the kids. Oh, they would love you. We always talked about getting a dog. It just was never the right time. I'm glad you're here, girl. I don't think I would enjoy doing this alone. You'll meet Jacqui and my kids one day soon. When this is all over. You'll love them. And they'll love you. They're always fussing over dogs we pass in the street. I haven't told you the names of my kids have I?"

Skye's focus was anywhere but on Eric, but that didn't stop the one way conversation. He need it.

"Luke and Katie. I don't think you'd get tired of their attention. They'll want you sleeping in their rooms, but we'll put an end to that idea before it starts. No sleeping in the bedrooms, okay? We'll get you a comfortable bed, and set it up right next to my arm chair. And when we go out on our walks, they won't be anything like this. I've seen enough snow for a lifetime. We have tree-lined streets and parks. Do you chase balls, Skye? Yep, you'll enjoy being part of our family."

Eric wiped his forehead. "We just need to keep going, girl. I don't want to die out here. If we keep going we'll be alright. One foot in front of the other. We can do it. Come on, Skye."

They kept away from the road, but were close enough to see abandoned vehicles, many buried beneath snow to the windows. The cold was taking a toll. Eric felt it in his bones, and not even the exertion of moving to combat the resistance of the snow warmed him enough to stop his teeth chattering. Skye stopped often waiting for Eric to catch up. Yes, he'd take her home to meet his family when this was all over, and make sure she had a bed as soft as the one the Ingram's had provided her.

A sign was nailed to a tree up ahead. Words in large red letters. *FOR SAFETY AND SURVIVAL FOLLOW RED MARKERS.*

Beneath the sign, a length of red fabric flailed manically.

"Well, we're on the right track, Skye." Eric drew the lapels of his borrowed coat to his chin. "Not far to go," he said with hope.

The weather worsened, his progress slowed, but the red markers kept appearing. He paused on the crest of a small hill, shielding his eyes from the wind and powdery snow. Skye shook herself free of snow then bit at compacted formations that hung from her hair. The last red marker he had spotted lay two miles behind. Lone trees punched up through the snow, their bare branches stretching to the sky. A low, stone wall snaked down and away from him. A farm or village must be nearby. Only a few more hours of daylight remained.

"A roof over our heads soon," he said to Skye.

The dog blinked away the snow falling, as if suggesting she didn't believe him.

"Well, there better be."

They reached the wall. A thin trench followed the line of the wall suggesting the path well-trodden recently. Skye's ears pricked up.

Eric threw himself down, eating a face full of snow, and pulled his weapon free. "Down, Skye."

Two figures clad in white were on the summit and moving downhill. Their attire rendered them near invisible and they seemed to glide on the snow, moving far quicker than Eric could in these conditions.

Skye let out a low growl. The two figures held their position, one scanning downhill with binoculars. For an impossibly long time, their gaze seemed to lock onto Eric. He pushed himself further into the snow, rocking his body to dig himself further depth.

The two figures moved again and fast. They were on skis. Eric aimed his firearm. Skye growled again. They pulled up a hundred feet before Eric.

"Ho! Survivor!" said one, and raised a hand in greeting. He had a hunting rifle with a long barrel slung over his shoulders. "We're here to help."

The other said, "You won't need your gun. You're safe here." It was a female's voice.

The wind whistled and whipped up snow.

"I'm looking for a place for the night," shouted Eric. "You know anywhere nearby?"

The man pulled his scarf down, exposing his mouth. "You're looking for the military camp? Of course you are, why else would you be out here?"

"The markers ended awhile back. I've been stumbling around out here. Are we close?"

"Can we approach?"

Eric waved them forward and stood. He kept his AR-15 to hand. Skye wagged her tail then growled softly.

"Stay, girl."

"My name is Arvid and this is my wife Camilla. We're from the military camp." A Scandinavian accent.

"I'm Eric Mann." His body shook with the cold, his teeth continued to chatter.

"You've been out in this for some time. And who is your companion?" Camilla tapped her leg, beckoning Skye to her.

Skye hesitated, her tail wagging. She was obeying Eric's order, but keen to meet their new companions.

"We've been having issues with the markers disappearing," said Arvid. "The wind."

Eric didn't respond. Skye was still at his side.

"My wife and I sweep this area every day. You're not the first to be lost out here. Sometimes it's too late."

"We shouldn't linger out here," said Camilla.

"Is it far?"

"A half-hour."

Skye's tail wagged quickly. She seemed to be telling Eric not to fear these people, and Eric knew he had little choice.

"Go on, girl," he said, and Skye headed off to say her hellos.

Camilla petted the dog and spoke sweetly to her.

"Her name's Skye," he explained.

"Oh, and you're as pretty as a sky, Skye," Camilla crooned. Skye had found a new friend. She walked in circles with her excitement.

"Can you tell me a little about the camp?" said Eric.

"Of course," said Arvid. "We can talk as we travel. This way."

Eric followed them back up the hill.

"Do you know much about the outbreak?" asked Arvid.

"Some."

"My wife and I were caught up in it long before the media warned everyone. Luckily, we were swept up with a multinational military force. They were establishing this camp and had orders to collect survivors and hold them until arrangements could be made to move them to safe zones. And here we are. Alive."

"How many people have been taken in?"

"A few hundred. We were broadcasting the position but our equipment was damaged. We've put signs around the roads hoping to draw people to us."

"And the safe zones?"

"We've yet to hear about them. For now, we're well supplied. The weather is our ally. It keeps the infected away for the most part. Oh, they'll chase someone through the snow without hesitation and it barely slows them down, but we've noticed a decrease in strays coming out this way when the weather is particularly bad."

"What about other groups of survivors? There must be others? Not just here but in the rest of the country."

"Until recently, yes. We were in communication with them. But the cities are now lost. The advice to stay put doomed so many."

"Do you have family?" asked Camilla. Her eyes were blue and caring.

"Yes. I left them before things became this bad. They had a safe house to get to."

"Have you heard from them?" asked Arvid.

"No."

"I am sure they are well," said Camilla.

***

The camp was not as Eric had imagined. From a distance it was little more than a cluster of trees, barely deserving the description of a wood. It sat atop a gentle hill. Smoke clung above the treetops. Far from being a fully operational fenced and secure military installation, he found a group of survivors carving out a corner of hope. Arvid held up a red scarf as they approached.

"Signals survivors are approaching," she explained. "We have a few outposts to pass."

The outposts were set up at regular intervals on the slope of the hill. At the first outpost, a soldier leapt from his foxhole, levelling his rifle at Eric.

"Hands up and surrender your weapons."

"Hey, easy soldier," said Arvid. "He's with us. I've told him he can keep them."

"You know the rules, Arvid."

Arvid nodded. "Better than most, but I've given my word. That is enough. Okay?"

The soldier waved them through, Arvid's word going a long way it seemed. No further challenges were received from the other outposts.

Beyond the outposts trenches, little more than ditches, ringed the site. Men in thick clothing dug at a slow pace. Armed men walked the perimeter.

"It's a tough task, digging in the frozen earth," said Arvid. "It's all done by hand. Everyone here takes a turn to dig the defences. Everyone who is able. That's key to this place. If you're able, you contribute. Even something as mundane as digging a hole can make a difference."

"I want to speak with the base commander," said Eric.

"He's a very busy man," explained Arvid. "Very few get to speak directly to him."

"Who is he?"

"Ah! That's for someone other than me to tell."

"Why?"

"And that's another query to be dealt with by another."

They proceeded over a section of trench. Within the confines of the small forest, a sea of tents awaited. Many were uniformed, dull-green in colour. Military issue. Cheap, mass-produced shelters, the kind that the UK may have donated to disasters abroad. Now, they needed them at home. Yet there were also some of the kind that were found in households, packed away for summers that never came. Containers and military vehicles were stored to the far side. The tall trees dispersed the smoke emanating from the many fires.

Daylight was fleeing. People exchanged greetings with Arvid and Camilla, and many gravitated toward Skye and fussed over her. Skye loved it. She was gifted small bites of food while Eric received reserved nods and wary glimpses. The military element of the camp seemed to be comprised of many nations. Uniforms from the UK, France, USA and Germany.

"Why don't we find you a tent and you can rest?" said Camilla, her skis over her shoulder.

They walked further into the camp, through the trees and picked their way through the haphazard placements of tents. Small fires burned, some heating pots of water, others heating outstretched hands. A father and son tossed a ball to each other in the scant space between tents. Another man washed clothes in a bucket before passing them to his partner to hang them on a length of rope suspended between two trees. Some way off, sounds of a guitar were accompanied by claps and voices from those who sang along to the tune. A man stood over a pile of logs. He wiped his brow, leaning on his axe.

"So this is our tent. It's where we call home for the time being."

Outside Arvid and Camilla's tent was an intricate fire pit. A Dakota Fire Hole. To the untrained eye, it was little more than a hole, twelve inches wide and ten inches deep. Above the main hole, a metal grill was placed for cooking on. It was designed to produce minimal smoke. It was unlit. Beside the fire pit, a collection of camping seats waited. In happier times families may have sat around the campfire, melting marshmallows, sharing stories, and sipping on beers. There were four seats, not two. Perhaps camp life here encouraged a measure of normality and communication and friendships.

"And that can be your home for the time being, Eric." Arvid pointed to a tent not twenty feet away. No fire pit. No chairs. "It's empty now."

"Now? What happened to the previous resident?"

"They decided to leave. Get some rest, Eric. I'll bring you some hearty food in a few hours. Tomorrow we'll get you registered as an official resident of the camp."

No fires burned near Eric's tent but the grouping of trees provided a wind break of sorts, and lessened the chill that threatened to swallow him whole. He unzipped the front of the tent, pulling the flap aside. Inside were two thick sleeping bags with accompanying bedrolls, and a change of clothes that would have served a male and female couple, two drinking flasks and a lamp.

Eric crawled inside. "Come on, girl. It's a little warmer in here."

Skye entered, her footing cautious, her nose working even harder identifying the new scents. She appeared and slipped inside the tent, also. He removed his outerwear and stored his weapons by the bedside. He pulled his boots free, and tucked himself into the sleeping bag. He threw one of the blankets over Skye who happily curled up next to him. There was little noise outside. Exhaustion was ready to take him. Eric lay back, using his pack as a pillow. The tent flap was pulled aside and a thoughtful camp member slipped in a large dish of water.

"I think you'll like it here, girl."

***

Hector Crispin sat in his chair, head in his hands like a morose king enthroned. All efforts to restore communication with Captain Mathers in Glasgow had failed. Ryan waited for him to say something, and more so to excuse him, send him away.

A clock ticked marking the passing seconds. In the dullness of the room the man's eyes glistened, betraying his poker face. Hector picked up his glass using both hands when the tremors threatened to overcome control. He sipped at the drink.

Ryan was little more than a silent witness to the man's alcoholism. The idea that Hector had a daughter surprised Ryan. There were no personal items in the office, no family pictures to indicate friendships, relationships or family, and certainly no daughter. But Ryan imagined her to be beautiful, and a little older than him. Perhaps they could form some sort of bond. If she was hot, so much the better. She'd be intelligent, clever and forthright, cunning and ruthless. Her voice would be like a sharp politician's. But what if she looked like Hector? What if she drank like him? What if she was overweight? Ryan wondered what her name could be. Sally? No, that was a name for dolls and cats. Marsha? No, too much like a party girl. Anastasia? Yes, that sounded like a name Hector would bestow on his child. And the name Anastasia Crispin held a certain charm. Anastasia Bannister sounded good, too.

Hector set down the glass with a clunk. "We'll talk again soon, Ryan."

Ryan didn't waste any time lest Hector withdrew the dismissal. He opened the door and shrugged at the waiting Law. Ryan tried to give off an air of intimacy with Hector. He pinned a forlorn look on his face, but Law simply pushed past him.

"Law, I wonder if you could have our forces in Glasgow prepare a drone flyover of the facility. I want to know what we're up against. Put them on alert for immediate action, too."

Law closed the door.

Whoever was trying to take over the facility in Glasgow was going to discover the extremes of The Owls of Athena's retribution.

**

Brutus stormed down the corridor. He decided to do this alone for it would require his singular way of thinking. He reached the cells, scanned the keycard and stepped inside. The woman backed up against a wall. Brutus pulled the two bound men out of the cell, kicked the door closed on the woman, then marched them into the freezing corridors. The two men were frail, frightened, reluctant to move, but Brutus's persuasive hold had them moving. They reached the storage chamber and made straight for the industrial freezers.

"Please don't," said one of the prisoners.

"You are about to learn that I do not understand the concept of mercy." Brutus pushed both men into the cold unit, slammed the doors and left them to freeze. It would take no more than thirty minutes.

Brutus returned to the cells. The woman was crouched on the floor, her arms wrapped around her torso.

"What have you done with them?" Her voice was quiet, but with a distinct certainty.

Outside the cell hung a padded coat on a peg. Brutus pulled it free and threw the garment at the feet of the woman. She regarded it with suspicion before standing and putting it on, zipping it high.

The woman was slim, tanned, short blonde hair pulled back into a tight ponytail. She wore no make-up. She didn't need any. She possessed a natural beauty and her alert, blue eyes suggested a sharp intelligence.

"Nobody is coming to help you," said Brutus flatly. "All attempts of The Owls of Athena to take control here have failed. I am in control. This place is mine. Your associates are thirty minutes away from death. Their survival is completely up to you. Understand?"

The woman remained silent.

"Nobody is coming to help you, bitch."

She began to laugh, a low snarky sound. "I don't think you appreciate the seriousness of your situation."

"I don't think *you're* appreciating *your* situation."

"You've walked into your grave, whoever you may be. It's just a matter of time. I am Helena Crispin. My father is Hector Crispin. And he is the man that will ensure you die in the most horrendous way."

"Really?" Brutus pulled his combat knife from its scabbard. "I wonder what your father would give to have you back and in what condition."

Brutus placed the blade of the knife to her throat. She turned her head away, closing her eyes, jaw clenched tight.

"You are a means to an end. I've plans for this place, plans that don't involve you, your old bastard father, nor any of his Owls of Athena. You make yourself useful to me and you might just walk out of here alive, if not unspoiled."

With the tip of the blade Brutus undid her coat's zip, and lowered further until the blade was at the point between her breasts. He pushed until her face contorted.

"I realised long ago that life was fragile and ultimately worthless. It's far easier taking a life than it is to build one. Killing you means nothing. Letting you live takes effort. For now, you're worth my effort." Brutus withdrew the knife. "You'll have access to food, water and warmth. For now." He sheathed his weapon. "I'll have one of my men see to your comfort, Miss Crispin."

She lifted her chin. Her mettle had returned. "What about the others?"

Helena Crispin was an asset and for the moment she was useful. He would kill her yet. The length of her life depended on how useful she remained. Brutus almost wished that she was redundant to his cause.

"Has thirty minutes passed?"

***

"What's he doing?" Jacqui stood beside Jane, both women peering out the window.

"Digging," supplied Jane. "He's been digging traps in the trees. He's pushing himself hard."

Carter was in the treeline that marked the boundary of the house, hacking at the earth between the trees with a short spade. A small oil lamp sat on the earth.

"He doesn't seem himself lately," said Jacqui. "I don't know what it is but something's changed with him. I can see it behind his eyes. Since getting here, he's different."

"You know him better than I do," said Jane. "You think it's the Crosslys being here that's done it?"

Jacqui shook her head. "No. It's what's happening out there. I think it would make even the most resolute bend a little." Jacqui rested her forehead against the windowpane. "If Eric was here ..." She let the thought go unfinished.

"Oh, Jacqui. I'm sorry. I didn't mean to upset you. You know Eric is fine."

"Yes. He's still alive. If he were dead I'd know it. He's gone through worse and come back to us."

Jane placed an arm around Jacqui and pulled her close.

"We better check the fire in the living room," said Jane. "If Eric's out there looking after the world, the least we can do is look after the people around us."

The Crosslys slept in the living room clustered around the fire. The doors to the bedroom were open so Jacqui could keep an eye on the kids. When the fire was blazing, a healthy heat spread from the living room to the bedroom. But it was now burning low, and Jane would not let it go out. The fire was what kept them alive. Katie and Luke slept soundlessly with blankets heaped upon their small bodies, but the coming cold would be sure to wake them.

"Food's going to be an issue. There's not enough for everyone."

Jane agreed. "We've enough canned food and long life stuff to last a little. Guess we never anticipated having more mouths to feed."

They would eventually need to leave the house and risk the berserk world out there. But that was a problem to ponder another night.

"You should get some sleep, Jacqui. I'll stoke the fire, then I'll stay up a bit and make sure Carter is okay."

Jacqui squeezed Jane, let her go, crossed into the bedroom and climbed into bed. She extended a protective arm over the two kids.

The infected terrified Jane. The lack of food worried her. But she was growing more concerned at Carter's behaviour. He seemed to have become so single minded in his approach to the situation. The digging continued.

***

Freddo and Taylor kept watch on the walls. Brutus and the other men were in the communication room. The mood was sombre. Magnus busied himself with a pair of headphones and jotted notes onto a notepad, the scraping of pencil on paper the only sound. Murray stood off to the side by the doorway, arms folded, ill at ease in the company of grieving soldiers. Niall watched the floor, elbows on his knees. Ash Gibbons munched on a chocolate bar. Magnus, standing with his back against the wall volunteered to work at the communications station, attempting to glean useful information about the world in which they now existed.

"So what now?" asked Niall. "The infected at our door, and there are a lot of weapons out there with the dead."

"We'll collect them soon," said Brutus. "The convoy was carrying a lot of equipment we can use. As for the infected, let them pound on the walls all they like. There's no way for them to get inside. We need full schematics for the building. We need to know how everything works. And we need to figure out what we have and what we need. The storage vault is under stocked by half."

"We need more people," said Niall. "We don't have enough to guard the walls and make this place work."

"And where do you suggest we get those people from, people willing to work for us?" Freddo asked. "People aren't lining up for employment anymore."

"There must be people in Glasgow still. Offer them a safe haven and they will come."

"Silas says he has a small group of men in hiding in the city," said Brutus.

"And we believe him? We trust him?" asked Freddo.

"No."

Ash stuffed the chocolate bar wrapper into a pocket. "What about Niall's idea? Doesn't seem too bad a suggestion to me."

"You saw The Owls scum filtering back into the city," said Freddo. "We send out an open invitation and we'll wake up with our throats slit."

"Guys, I might have just found the answer." Magnus pulled his headphones free, hurriedly wrote a few further notes then spun in his chair. "Whoever was manning this station before we came along transcribed a shit load of radio broadcasts. They marked them with times and dates. There's a military base set up as a civilian collection north of here. They were broadcasting up until a few days ago."

"Maybe it's been overrun." Niall scanned the notes Magnus made. "Why wouldn't they be broadcasting now?"

"No signal. But this is the best bit of information I've been able to scrounge so far. They've supplied the location in the radio messages. It's around ninety miles from here."

"Jesus, Magnus," said Ash. "How are we supposed to get ninety miles? We can barely go outside the walls without being ripped apart or gunned down. And you're wanting us to go off on some crusade for a place that might not even exist?"

"We can fly," said Magnus.

"Yeah, the helicopter," suggested Murray.

"And of course we all know how to fly the damned thing," Ash mocked.

"Silas is a pilot." Brutus felt the need for some air. "Magnus, try to establish communication with the camp. If we can speak to them, I'll consider your suggestion. Niall, have Freddo help you collect the gear outside the walls. Ash, find me the schematic plans for the building. I want to know everything about this place. No secrets. No room for error. Once we've done this we can sort out where we'll be living. I want us all on the same floor. It's been a long goddamned day."

Brutus climbed the stairs to the top floor and out onto the helipad. He sat down at the edge, letting his legs dangle over the side. No lights gave his position away. Beyond his immediate confines, the city of Glasgow burned. He wondered how many good people remained. Not many, he guessed. The good died off quickly and the evil bastards lingered on, surviving like a virus. Well, it was a virus, he reminded himself. Brutus pulled a cigar from his breast pocket and lit it. The rain was little more than drizzle.

Brutus smoked and watched a city die.

CHAPTER 10

THE BONES OF A DYING WORLD

On his first full day, Eric was stripped down and examined for signs of infection by a soldier who appeared to possess only rudimentary medical experience. His pupils were checked for responses, and a thermometer was inserted into his ear. He was registered in the most basic way: name, date of birth, blood type, physical appearance. His picture was taken on a digital camera. He was shown around the camp.

"That trench over there is the camp's latrine," explained his guide. The old man walked with a slow gait. He touched at lanterns hanging from tree branches. "We light these at dark. Helps to see where you're going at night. No use tripping up and causing more headaches for the medical team."

"Medical team? What medical team?"

"Good question. And over there," he said pointing north, "that's the command tent."

"I want to speak to those in charge."

He chuckled. "If they feel the need to speak with you, you'll be summoned. Got to be of importance to talk to them. But they do alright. At least we're functioning. We're all contributing in one way or another. What can you do?"

"Whatever's needed."

In the first week of camp life Eric quickly grew accustomed to the rhythm of his new everyday life. The civilian population gathered every second day to discuss camp life and to bring any points of contention or question to those in charge. Most issues arose from dwindling supplies, and what was needed and what there was plenty of, and organising work details for the defences. The meetings lasted an hour. Attendance was not mandatory but was encouraged. Despite the pain at his ribs, Eric dug the trenches each day. He asked several officers about making use of his specialised skillsets but met with the same answer. It wasn't their call to make.

The children in camp called him Dog Man and Skye proved to be a welcome addition. She would often go running off to enjoy the affections others lavished on her. The kids threw sticks for her to fetch, or they'd simply lie down on the ground and encourage Skye to snuggle next to them while they petted her stomach. After the first week people were less guarded, opening up, chatting more freely. Eric listened to tales of survival. Every person in the camp had a harrowing story. A great many were swept up by the military in their rush to establish the camp. Some told stories of hiding in their homes until hunger compelled them to move, and seeing signs to the camp or hearing radio broadcasts. Some arrived after wandering aimlessly, only chance bringing them to safety. Everyone lost somebody.

The military elements of the camp were polite and professional. Helpful, but vigilant. Eric built a fire pit outside his tent, and collected his own firewood from the forest floor, and fashioned his own cooking equipment from pieces donated to him by other camp residents. He sat outside his tent on the only chair he possessed. A pot of water bubbled above the flames to make tea. Skye's barks were not far away. They were friendly barks. The camp kids must have been keeping her busy again with sticks or balls. On the air, someone cooked meat of some kind. The military was adept at living off the land. Several snares were set up around the immediate area. Birds were brought down from the trees. Rabbits were caught further out from camp. So far, only occasional trips out far were needed to raid for supplies.

"Dog Man?"

A teen girl stood above him.

"Some people call me that," he said. "Mostly kids. It's Eric."

"Eric Mann, I know. You're wanted over in the command tent. I'll show you the way."

"I know where it is. I'll find my way."

"Sorry, but I was told to bring you. Follow me."

Eric stood, grabbed his weapon and followed the girl. They navigated through the camp. A ripple of laughter sounded to their left. The sound was a rarity in camp. Skye appeared at his side, panting heavily from her play. They passed a pair of Warrior vehicles. A soldier worked on one, his hands black with grease.

"Straight up there," she said, pointing to a path that passed through a wall of containers and more military hardware.

"As I said, I know."

"Whatever," said the girl turning her back and walking away.

A large green pavilion tent waited ahead. A soldier stood outside, a sidearm at his hip.

He held the flap open for Eric to enter. "Dog's to stay outside."

"Stay, Skye."

Inside two men waited, sitting behind a frail table, the kind that might be used for pop-up stalls. One man wore the insignia of a Major. The other, a middle-aged man, his greying hair slicked back, wore a suit jacket and an open shirt. He made a triangle with his fingers. The triangle collapsed as he stood and he held out a hand.

"Ah, you must be Eric."

"Some call me Dog Man."

"So I've heard."

The men shook hands and Eric sat in the offered chair. The two men returned to sitting on the other side of the table.

"Do you know who I am, Eric?"

"No, I don't. Have we met before?"

"No, we haven't. I'm Alex Cunningham. I'm Scotland's Secretary of State. For all intents and purposes I am the civilian authority in this camp, and this is Major Reid."

The Major nodded a greeting.

"It's filtered back that you have been requesting a meeting with us, so given your persistence we thought we owed it to you. And we've heard that dog of yours is quite popular around camp."

"Skye," Eric provided.

"Perhaps first, a little information about yourself, if you please."

Major Reid was the quiet one, but Eric felt him studying his every move more intently than Alex Cunningham.

"I was employed with Black Aquila until things fell apart."

"Black Aquila?"

"A private security firm that worked with the DSD in Aberdeen."

Alex looked to the Major. "You were in Aberdeen?"

"I was. Before that we were operational in Iraq. We were rendered ineffective after Aberdeen. Too many people died for too little gain. I was back home, just outside London before everything went to shit. My family is still down there."

"How did you get up here?"

Eric detailed his task to search for Gemma, the helicopter crash, his stay on the farm and his escape, all the way up to spotting the skiers in the snow. He left little out. Eric finished, saying, "I wouldn't have left my family if I had known the real situation."

Alex whipped off his glasses and rubbed his forehead. "You're angry and you've every cause to be that way. The main reason for this place is to collect survivors, protect them until such a time as safe zones can be set up. At the moment, no zones have been identified. There is no functioning government. Other elements of our armed forces are setting up camps like this. For now, we're on our own and can't expect reinforcement or additional supplies until order is maintained. That takes time. We're reeling but not defeated."

"How is London?"

Major Reid answered, "London is lost. Our projections are that ninety percent of the population has fallen to the Carrion Virus. All elements of the armed forces have been ordered to disperse and work toward setting up safe zones where they can protect those left."

"What about the wider world?"

Alex said, "India and Pakistan are in a state of all-out war. There have been clashes in the DMZ in Korea, artillery exchanges. It's like the virus has opened the floodgates to all the world's issues. The middle-east has pretty much gone silent from what I understand. In America, the cities are all but a nest of the infected. Like us, they've been moving forces to rural locations. As for the rest of the world, we just don't know."

"So what is your plan, Eric?" asked Major Reid.

"To get back to my family and then survive. I'm willing to work toward that. If I can help out here, I will."

"That's no small task. It's not as easy as picking up a phone or taking a flight across the country. Information is hard to come by. Half the people in this camp are missing someone and want to be elsewhere. For the moment that is not possible," said Alex.

"I know that," said Eric. "Yet finding them is what's keeping me alive. May I ask a question?"

The Secretary of State indicated he should go on.

"What if you're the highest ranking official in government still alive?"

"If we can establish that, then Major Reid and I will work on certain plans to put into effect. I can tell you're a useful man to have here, Eric. We're planning to replenish certain supplies in the coming days. Perhaps you can go along. I feel your talents are wasted digging the defences of our camp."

"Like I said, I'm willing to help while I'm here."

"Then we'll talk again soon."

Eric stood.

"One thing before you go," said Major Reid. "What do you know of The Owls of Athena?"

"I've heard rumours they're the ones responsible for all this."

"Nothing else?"

"No."

"Thank you. You may leave," said the Major.

Eric walked from the tent, leaving the soldiers behind. Skye followed. He thought it best to keep his limited knowledge of The Owls to himself, especially their infiltration of Black Aquila and the DSD. At least for now. Trust was a rare commodity these days. Alex Cunningham and Major Reid seemed to be decent men but time would reveal if Eric was correct or otherwise.

"Eric? Oh my God, it is you. Eric!"

***

They drove for over an hour before finding a retail park, and bounced over a grass verge avoiding abandoned cars that blocked the entrance. The carpark made for grim viewing. It was littered with dead. Hundreds of them. There was a choking smell of death. Crows hopped between the bodies, their beaks busy.

Jane crouched behind an abandoned car, Carter next to her. Behind them, Harold and Elliot Crossly. After a week of relying on the meagre supplies they brought with them, it was time to venture out and gather more. Harold and his son and Jane accompanied Carter, and Jacqui remained at the house with Isabelle and the kids. Carter insisted Jacqui carry two sharp kitchen knives with her at all times. Isabelle pleaded with Carter to let Elliot remain but he would not relent.

"He's not a young child. He can earn his keep, and that of his family."

Isabelle hugged Elliot tightly before they left.

"Remember," urged Carter to his companions, "you do as I say and we get out of this in one piece. You don't listen and go running off nobody will risk themselves bringing you back. Understand?"

"Mr. Carter, you won't have any bother from us. All we want to do is our part. My son and I want to pay back the kindness you've shown since we've met. If we can be of service out here, we will. I understand you're a man of experience."

"And just remember that if the shit hits the fan."

Jane tailed Carter moving to another abandoned closer to the shops. Harold and Elliot scuttled up from the behind.

"Look's deserted," Harold said. "That's good."

"No." Carter did not take his eyes off the front of the shop. "Those things are clever. They won't wait out in poor weather. They seek shelter when they need it. The entire shop could be a nest of them."

Much of the glass facade was cracked or smashed. The security shutter was buckled and suspended.

"Then why don't we head back? We could search those houses we passed," suggested Harold.

"I doubt we'd find anything we can use."

A distant rumble rang out overhead.

"You hear that?" said Jane.

"It's been raining pretty hard," said Harold. "Wouldn't surprise me if we got some thunder and lightning at some point."

"Aircraft," said Carter. "Flying low."

All three looked to the sky. Two fighter jets roared overhead, the noise loud enough to make Jane sink to her knees. Two helicopter gunships appeared, moving slower and at a lower altitude. Elliot pushed himself between Jane and his father.

"We're still in this," said Harold, striking a fist to the sky. "We're still fighting."

Carter pulled Harold's fist down. "Look about you, asshole. You see everyone dead in this carpark? How many do you think there are? Hundreds? Close to five-hundred? The infected didn't do all this. Skulls blasted apart by high-powered weapons. Children blown from their mother's arms and gunned down. Infected don't shoot guns. It's them up there." He pointed heavenward. "They can't recognise friend from foe right now."

"Carter, maybe right now isn't the best time to be a prick," said Jane.

"No! It's the perfect time to be a prick. It's time he realises this is the world we live in now. All this is what to expect day in day out. There's no place for being timid. Those who are end up dead or worse."

"Stop. Please," pleaded Elliot.

"And you, you little streak of piss. You want to go on living? You need to be prepared to do what it takes out here."

Jane stood and walked from the cover of the car.

"Jane! Get back here!" Carter leapt the bonnet of the car and caught up with her. "Are you deaf?"

"I don't want to hear any more of your bullshit bullying, Carter. What the hell's the matter with you? I'm going in. I'll grab what I can and we can be out of here."

Carter seized her arm. "You'll do what I tell you."

Jane pulled free, grabbed the Glock from her coat and pointed it at Carter's face. "I swear to God if you lay another hand on me in that fashion, you'll regret it." The gun felt heavy. She had never pulled a trigger before. Her fingers fidgeted trying to discover the correct way to hold it. It felt awkward. She felt clumsy.

Carter snatched the weapon from Jane's ill-prepared grasp. "This isn't a game," he said. "I'm trying to keep you alive. Don't piss about with this. I know how to survive out there." He held the gun out to her, handle first.

Her hands shook.

"Take it. You might need it in there."

She did, and those shaking hands returned the gun to her pocket. "I'm sorry."

"No, you're not. Go and find supplies if you're so determined."

Jane blinked, then opened her mouth to snap back. But instead of cursing, she turned and ran to the door of the shop. She picked her way through the dead. So many. So many lives lost. None showed signs of infection. Many were in poor condition, ravaged by gunfire and by birds or other animals. Some still clung to their bags of meagre possessions. They died together, clustered close. Carter was right, many seemed to have been executed or riddled with indiscriminate gunfire. Death did not usually bother her. Being a nurse installed some professional desensitisation. But this, this was horror.

Jane tapped the shutter with the Glock three times then waited. Nothing. She ducked beneath the crumpled shutter. Glass crunched beneath her feet. She pulled a torch from her pocket and clicked it to life. A narrow beam shot out enough for her to navigate by. Cash tills were open and notes and coins sat untouched in their compartments. Funny how at the beginning of the outbreak people sought out money. Now it was a worthless reminder.

Jane pulled off her backpack and grabbed two long-life bags at the end of one of the checkouts. There wasn't a lot on the shelves but whatever was left would have to do. The days of picky eating were over. Jane swept her arm across a shelf, dumping tins into the bags. She found cereal boxes and squashed them into the second bag. More tins. More small packets.

A noise halted her movements. It was like someone tenderising meat, hammer blow after hammer blow into soft meat. She pulled the torch to her chest plunging the aisle into darkness. Her heart raced. The sound came from a few aisles away. She placed the bags on the ground, and the torch into a pocket, and fished out the Glock. It felt just as heavy and just as awkward as it had earlier. Her finger felt for the trigger. The noise stopped, but the shop fell too quiet. She breathed deeply, her eyes darting in the dark. Something sniffed in the darkness. Close. She wanted to scream to Carter, but he wouldn't make it before the infected reached her.

She released one hand from the Glock and pulled the torch from her pocket and pointed the light to the end of the aisle. An infected filled the thin beam of light. It wore a store uniform, tattered and ripped. It sniffed again and turned to the light and focused on Jane. Its mouth opened, revealing bloodied teeth. Jane closed her eyes and pulled the trigger. She missed. The infected let out a howl and then a scream and charged. Jane dropped the torch, and squeezed the trigger again and again and again, stepping back with every shot.

A weight knocked her back. She dropped the gun and fell to the floor. The weight followed. The infected emitted a high-pitched sound. Its legs wiggled, and then it ceased all movement. Warmth trickled down along Jane's neck and chest. She pushed and pulled but couldn't climb free of the weight.

A light flicked on.

"You see what happens when you don't listen to me, Jane?"

"Carter, get it off! Quick. It's bleeding out on me."

"You got yourself into this mess, Jane."

"Please, Carter! I don't want it on me! Take it off!"

"You have to take it off yourself, Jane. You need to find a way to survive yourself. Remember, I'm a prick, and you know everything."

Jane summoned a hidden reserve of strength and pushed the bulk aside. She jumped to her feet. Carter ran his torch over her body.

"You bastard!"

"There's blood on your hands, some on your neck, and all over your clothes."

"You could have helped me!"

"Yet you believe you know better than me." Carter retrieved the Glock from the floor, and kicked the torch back over to Jane. "Did it bite you?"

"No."

"You should wash yourself down. Ditch those clothes."

"And wear what?"

"You're not coming with us covered in its blood."

"How long were you here for?"

"Long enough to see you should have been more careful."

"You piece of shit, you could have stopped this?"

"I can't always be there to save you. Strip down, wash yourself and find something in here to cover you up. On second thoughts, I should leave you here."

"I didn't swallow any of its blood, Carter. I wouldn't put you all at risk if I had."

Carter studied her from head to toe for a long time. "Get changed and cleaned up. You'll be wearing restraints in the car. I'll have Jacqui check you twice a day for infection."

***

"It's really you." Gemma flew into Eric's arms, and clung to him as if her life depended on it. Tears rolled down her cheeks and onto his shoulder. He had saved her before. He would save her again. "What are you doing here?"

Eric pulled her away. His eyes looked left and right and over her shoulder. "Come with me."

"Why? Eric—"

"Gemma, not here."

She looked behind, but no one seemed interested in their presence or their departure. What was he hiding from?

A dog trotted at his heels.

"Your dog?"

"Skye. And yes, I suppose she is mine."

"Here, Skye."

The dog padded over to her, its tail wagging, and accepted a scratch on its head.

"Where are we going?"

"Away from ears."

They walked to the edge of the forest at the camp boundary. Eric turned, his eyes searching for company. Gemma checked, too. No one. The wind bit at her nose. She wrapped her arms across her body.

"Why are you here?"

"To get you home. Williamson sent me."

Skye sniffed at the air, decided it was too cold and plodded off back to the tents and campfires.

Eric frowned and grinned. "You do remember asking to be rescued?"

"Yes, of course I do. It's just been a time since then, and, well I thought they forgot about me."

"Nothing happens quickly anymore, Gemma."

"Yeah, so I'm learning. How did you know I was here?"

"I didn't. The aircraft I was travelling in went down."

"What?" She looked him up and down expecting to find signs of an air crash survivor. But what did she expect to find? "You're okay?"

"Yes. An older couple found me and took me in. An infected turned up at their home."

"They're dead?"

"They're dead."

"And that's where you got Skye?"

Eric nodded. A blackbird landed on a branch above their heads, and dislodged some snow. It slapped on Gemma's head.

She looked up and laughed. "Good shot," she said to the bird.

Eric released a tired smile. "Your laughter is a pleasure to hear."

"Yeah, not much of it around here."

"No. But how did you end up here? I was told to find you at the hospital."

"I didn't think anyone was coming, so I left the hospital, got lost, found an empty house and a map directing me here."

"I've not seen you around the camp."

"I've been out on patrol. They're trying to set up an outpost fifteen miles from here."

"You volunteered?"

"You're surprised?"

"No. No, Gemma. I'm not surprised at all."

"I was with soldiers. They kept me safe."

"What do you make of Alex Cunningham?"

"Alex? From what I can gather, he's a decent man in an impossible situation."

"And Major Reid?"

"I've barely spoken to him. Why?"

"Did they ask you about The Owls of Athena?" Eric almost whispered the group's name like it was a curse.

"No. I've heard the name, but no, I haven't been asked. They don't look at me as very important. Who are The Owls of … whatever their name is?"

"The Owls of Athena. Perhaps best you don't know."

"Eric!"

"Trust me, Gemma."

Gemma shrugged in resignation. "I have no choice, do I?"

"No. And don't volunteer any information, not until I get a handle on the situation."

"But nothing here strikes me as off. These people, they're trying to help, trying to foster hope and preserve something of what we've lost. There's goodness here. I've seen it."

The blackbird launched itself from its perch and flew away.

"Can we head back? I'll freeze if I stand still any longer."

They started back the way they came, Gemma slipping her arm beneath Eric's. She was going to be fine. Eric would get her home safely. His presence made the world suddenly possess some order again.

***

Brutus contemplated the wisdom of taking a trip to the military camp. The helicopter gauge indicated fuel to be low, and he had no knowledge of supply opportunities out there.

He rubbed his chin and scanned his men. "Alright, you know the score. We've made contact with the military camp and we need to make a trip in the helicopter. A personal introduction serves two purposes. We can get a feel for who these people are, whether they can be of benefit or not. And they have supplies that we may need, that we can trade."

"Who's going?" asked Niall.

"Me and Silas. Everyone else is needed here. I don't expect to be gone more than a day or two."

Niall crushed a plastic cup and threw it into the bin. "And if Silas decides to pull one of his tricks?"

"Then he's a dead man."

"And then you're stuck at the camp unless you've taken flying lessons recently."

"One shit problem at a time," said Brutus.

"Who will be in charge when you're gone?" asked Taylor.

"Niall is in charge until I'm back. Magnus, let them know we're departing."

***

Flying over Glasgow revealed the true extent of the horror.

"I thought I'd seen everything there was to see in Iraq," said Silas through his headset. "But you look down there, and you know this world has changed. I am not sure if we are the lucky ones or not."

Brutus couldn't count the bodies down below even if he tried. "Less talk, more flying."

***

The frozen ground was unforgiving, but Eric liked the repetitive nature of the work. Digging trenches invited automatic movements, and allowed him to retreat into silence, a private retreat where he did not need to think too much. But pain compelled him to stop if only for a moment, pain at his ribs and pain in his hands. He threw down his shovel and pulled his gloves off. His hands were red and raw. It felt like a fire burned beneath his skin.

"Eric, isn't it?" One of his fellow diggers moved up next to him, dropping his tool, too. "Or Dog Man? That's what the kids have taken to calling you."

Eric tucked his gloves under his arm and shook the offered hand.

"I'm Mike Kazimier. Can we take five minutes to get our breath back?"

"I don't suppose it gets any easier?" he replied, looking back at his hands.

"I'm afraid not." Mike showed Eric his own blisters. "Nothing we can do about them. No pain, no gain, they say."

Mike sat down onto the edge of the trench, legs dangling over the edge. He pulled his canteen free and drank. Other workers followed, too, sat for a rest and water.

"I've heard them talking about mining the entire approach to this camp," said Mike. "There will be only one way in and one way out."

"Makes sense. Means we can concentrate firepower on the approaches."

"Makes sense until some poor bastard rushing toward the camp thinks they're saved, then *boom!*"

"That's what the outposts are designed to do, aren't they? Collect anyone looking for rescue and bring them back here?"

"Yeah, supposed to."

"How did you make it here, Mike?"

"I'm one of the lucky ones, got swept up with retreating military units. Life here for a start was hard. People died because we didn't have enough medical supplies, and we had to learn order. But it's gotten better. We all have a job to do. Everyone works. There's hope in the camp."

"Have you lost family?"

"Hasn't everyone? But my wife and kids are here. I'm blessed. As for the rest of my family and friends, I don't think it would be wise to hope. We've mourned them. What about you?"

"My wife and kids are out there somewhere. A friend is keeping watch over them."

Mike squeezed Eric's shoulder. "You'll see them again, my friend. Just not today. Today, we need to dig."

The men returned to their shovels and blisters.

***

Rain thudded against the window with enough force to rattle the glass. Jane lay on the bed, under two thick covers, shivering. It was dark. Carter gave Jacqui the task to attend to her, watch her closely. The door was not locked. Jane could walk out of the bedroom and leave the house. But there was nowhere to go. Not alone. Not anymore.

A light knock at the door brought her from her retrospect. She pushed herself up in the bed, pulling the covers to her chin. She was naked beneath by choice. As proof the Carrion Virus had not taken hold, she subjected herself to scrutiny.

"Jane, I'm not disturbing you am I?" Jacqui asked, carrying a small gas lamp as she entered.

"No, of course not. Is everything alright?"

Jane sat lightly on the edge of the bed. "Carter says the virus would have taken hold by now. You can come out."

Jane laughed a sound void of humour. "Carter knows if I had been infected I would have succumbed in a matter of minutes. An hour or two at the most. Being kept in here is punishment for what happened at the supermarket. It's bullshit. That's why the door isn't locked. Maybe he was hoping I would choose to leave. One less person to worry about."

"I don't know what happened there, Jane, but I know he was mad. He's said little to anyone since getting back. What did happen?"

Jane could have lied, but chose to be selective. "I thought I knew better. I didn't agree with Carter and went into the shop alone. I was silly and almost died."

"And Carter?"

"We all have our parts to play if we're going to make it. Carter has the military mind and he's best equipped to lead us."

She hated saying the words, it felt like colossal defeat.

"Don't downplay yourself, Jane. You're as valuable to this group as Carter or anyone else. We wouldn't have made it this far without you."

Jacqui patted her hand. Jane couldn't shake the feeling the gesture was more for her comfort than Jane's.

"Is everything okay, Jacqui? Are the kids okay?"

"It's not them. Carter brought back a few working radios and a stack of batteries. He's picked up transmissions, many transmissions. He says it's not safe for us to remain here much longer."

"But we've got food and supplies now, enough to last for weeks."

Jacqui shook her head. "It's not the food. It's something else. Get dressed. I'll make some tea." She placed the lamp on a table then closed the door behind her.

Jane dressed, grabbed the lamp and headed to the living room. The house was freezing. She was not sure of the time. The Crossley's slept bundled together on the floor, one of them snoring softly. Jacqui's children slept, too, wrapped tight in blankets. Carter sat at a table, large headphones on and connected to the radio. He tapped a pencil against the edge of the table as he listened. Jane touched Carter on the shoulder. He turned, not seeming surprised she was there. He pulled the headphones down.

"Jacqui said there's something wrong," she said in hushed tones.

"We might not be able to hole up here for much longer."

"What makes you say that?"

Carter pushed a small notepad to her and tapped it twice with the pencil. Jane placed her lamp next to the one on the table, picked up the notepad and leaned toward the light. It was a series of coordinates referencing a map. She was about to ask what they meant when Carter lifted the headphones back to his ear.

171

"He's broadcasting again. Listen."

Carter passed the headphones. Jane slipped them on. A voice and a background of static greeted her ears.

"My name is Mark Flood. If you're listening to this then you're alive. What I've got to say could keep you that way. What you're being told is a lie. The military are not looking to rescue survivors. There are elements of the military actively seeking out and eliminating pockets of survivors. I've seen this with my own eyes. The group I was with were killed with no warning as we begged for help. A few days ago we found a wounded soldier." A burst of static obscured his next words, and it faded again. "He confirmed they are operating in zones of outbreak. Anyone alive or infected within they've been instructed to kill. If you're in these zones you need to leave, and now. If you're looking for somewhere safe I can only offer this advice. Get as rural as you can. Stay off the roads. Avoid major population centres. And whatever you do, do not trust the military."

The broadcast broke down into static once more.

"The coordinates," said Jane. "We're in one of the zones of outbreak?"

Carter nodded. "We are. We're remote though. The chances of us being found right now is slim. And how long that goes on for, I'm not sure."

"Do we know who this Mark Flood is? Are you taking his threat seriously, Carter? It doesn't sound like the British Army to go around killing innocents."

"You saw the carpark and the bodies. And there is more than just the British involved here. Many nations sent help in the beginning."

"What if this Mark Flood is trying to get people to leave their hiding places and travel openly? They would make an easier target out in the open? What if he's a member of the military that's doing the killing? If we leave, we may be putting ourselves in further danger."

Carter rubbed his eyes and stifled a yawn. "Staying here was never a permanent solution. We were to come here and wait for Eric. I don't think he'll come here now. We need to consider options. We have food enough to make a journey but if we can't rely on the army for help, I don't know where we should make for. What do you think?"

"You're asking me?"

Carter sighed. "Jacqui thinks we should leave. She still believes Eric is alive and there will be chances to contact him somehow wherever we go."

"What about the Crosslys?"

He shook his head.

"Did you ask them?"

"No."

It felt like it wasn't the right choice, but circumstances were constantly robbing them of many choices which would have felt right.

"We're leaving aren't we, Carter?"

"Yes."

***

Eric made his way back to camp. The light was fading fast. All he wanted to do was sleep. He reached the clearing where his tent was pitched. Gemma was outside his tent, staring into an inviting fire. She was humming.

"Gemma?"

The humming stopped. "Welcome home, honey. How was your day?"

Eric sat down heavily and placed his rifle by his side. "Long and repetitive. I'm glad it's done."

"It'll be dark soon. I hate when it gets dark here. I've lived so long in the city that I've forgotten what it's like to be in total darkness. I hated it when I was a kid and now I find myself hating it as a grown ass woman. But the night never had real monsters in it back then." She picked up a can of beer, drank heavily then burped. "Oh excuse me," she said before laughing, then tossed the empty can to a pile. Four empty cans.

"Where did you get those from?"

"A girl has her ways," she said with a wink. "I have some for you."

She laughed again. Eric like the sound. She laughed like Jacqui. Completely and honestly. Gemma moved to his tent, pulled the flap back and returned with a six pack of beers. She pulled one free and tossed it to Eric. He caught it deftly, weighing it in his hands, and weighing up something else. Alcohol almost ruined everything for him. A lifetime ago, he self-medicated and it brought him to the edge. But that was when the world made a semblance of logic. He needed this. He needed an escape from the madness of the Carrion Virus, even if just for a night. He opened the can and took a long swill. It was cheap, domestic beer. But it would do.

"I heard a helicopter is arriving in camp later, someone from Glasgow. A group of survivors made contact."

"Good. Nice to know there are others out there." Eric drained the rest of his beer, crushed the can, threw it onto the pile Gemma had constructed and motioned for another. Gemma passed him one and he drank. The booze brought a welcome feeling to Eric's cold bones. Even his spine felt like it was thawing, and the muscles that had worked so hard out in the snow were beginning to relax.

"So what now?" he said.

"What do you mean?"

"Before all this Williamson was going to make you a famous reporter with your inside story on the outbreak. So what now?"

She brushed her hair back. "Why do you ask?"

"Conversation." He shrugged. "I'd talk about the weather if you'd prefer. It's cold. Really cold."

"Really, really cold," she added with a smile. But the smiled disappeared quickly. "Does anyone care how and why it all happened anymore? I mean really and truly? It *has* happened and we can't change that. So, no more famous journalist dreams for me. I want to get back to my parents. And, I spoke with Alex Cunningham this afternoon while you were out digging away. He said the bulk of our naval forces are still in operation. Can you believe that?"

"You got an audience with the camp boss?"

"Yep."

"How?"

"Like I said, I have my ways."

"You actually said, a girl has her ways."

"Whatever." Her smile returned. "But he has a plan to transfer survivors offshore and set up a colony on one of the islands. That's good news, yes?"

"Yes. It is." Eric kicked some twigs into the fire pit. Embers rose through the grill. "I'm not ashamed to confess that I'm scared, Gemma, scared to think I may not make it back to my family. They're five-hundred miles away but it may as well be on the other side of the planet."

"I believe we'll get home."

"You do?"

"Yeah. I have to."

He drained his second can and wiped his mouth with the back on his hand. Eric helped himself to a third, opened it and drank.

"Don't mind if I do," said Gemma grabbing herself another can. "You know, you've never told me much about your family?"

"My family?"

"Yeah."

Men walked through the camp lighting the lanterns that hung from branches.

"I have no idea where they are, nor whether they're safe or not, and we're sitting here drinking beer by a fire."

"No one knows much at the moment. So you're no different from everyone else here." One arm gestured to the other tents.

Eric shook his head, and studied the spitting flames. *Where are you, Jacqui? Are you worried about me, as I am about you and the kids?*

Gemma's hand found his. It was cold. "Things will be okay, I know it. You always make things right." Gemma shuffled closer. "Look at me, Eric."

Gemma looked nothing like Jacqui, but in that moment he saw a face that was able to put all thoughts of the current world to bed, if only for that short space in time. Jacqui could do that.

Gemma suddenly kissed him tenderly, and their lips remained touching for an inordinate time. Gemma snaked her arms around his neck, pulling him close. He responded, kissing her passionately.

They separated, breathing hard.

"Gemma, I think you've had a little too much to drink, and I … well, I can't do this."

"Shh. Don't talk." She stood, took his hand and led him into his tent, zipping it closed behind them.

Overhead, the pounding of a helicopter's engine broke the calm of the late evening.

***

Brutus waited to be admitted to the command tent. Two armed men blocked his way. Silas stood behind him with instructions to keep his mouth shut.

"Weapons," they demanded. "You'll get them back when you're done."

Brutus surrendered his guns and knife. "Look after them," he said, and stepped into the tent.

"Ah, you must be Brutus. I am Alex Cunningham."

Brutus nodded. "This is my pilot Mr. Salt."

"A pleasure," Alex said, shaking both men's hands then sitting.

"Please sit."

"We'll stand," said Brutus.

"If you wish," said Alex with a voice full of British eloquence. "I must admit your communication was a welcome surprise. There's little to celebrate these days, but contacting fellow survivors brings hope to us all."

"That's a nice helicopter," said Major Reid, suspicion dripping from his deep tone.

Brutus licked his lips. Respectful diatribe and negotiations were not his forte.

Alex cut in, "I understand you bring a proposal?"

Brutus said, "My associates and I have acquired a secure location within the city of Glasgow. It's safe from the infected. I offer shelter for your many survivors."

"And you want something in return?" said the Major.

"We are few in number. Your people would boast our security."

"They are not soldiers."

"They can be."

Alex said, "You've not mentioned who you and your associates are, or how you come to us."

"Yes, and armed with such an impressive rig," added the Major.

"I will, but I also bring you a warning."

"Yes?" Alex.

"The Owls of Athena."

Alex Cunningham and Major Reid looked to each other, then Alex walked from behind his desk.

"Well, Brutus, this facility you have, I'm intrigued. So please, go on."

"The Owls of Athena are enemy to all who survive. They're responsible for the virus, and they're coming for those who dare to defy them."

"And that is you?" asked Alex.

"And you."

"We can handle ourselves," said Major Reid.

Silas stepped forward. "With all due respect, I don't think you grasp the scope of their reach. They possess the resources to unleash a pandemic and bring the world to its knees, yet you believe they cannot destroy a makeshift camp such as yours?"

"Why would they?" asked the Major.

"Because of him," said Silas, pointing at Alex. "I know who you are, sir."

Alex lifted his chin. "Oh, do you now?"

Brutus would have knocked Silas out for talking then stomped on his head, but his words seemed to strike Alex where it mattered.

"I know your face. You might very well be the most senior member of government left alive. What you represent is order and that is the enemy of what they stand for. *You* could rally the surviving elements of the nation to fight back, and organisation is the enemy of their chaos."

The Major stepped forward. "We are monitoring the situation."

"Whatever your goals, as noble as they are, they put you at odds with The Owls of Athena," warned Silas. "Assume they are everywhere. Assume they know you are here. And assume they are coming for you."

"We're on the same side," said Brutus. "You and I, we're survivors but not for long without each other."

***

Helicopters had transported members of The Owls of Athena to the building, and they were guided to the top floor suite for a meeting.

The sat around a large, circular table. Ryan scribbled busily. His task was to take minutes, and Hector Crispin enjoyed extensive notes. Ryan's roles altered as Hector Crispin saw fit, and to describe him as Hector's personal assistant was close to the truth. Ryan ran errands, transcribed audio reports from the field, cooked, cleaned, and often in the evenings he was simply required to listen to Hector's ramblings, all whiskey induced. Ryan did not mind. It meant he was distant from the general population. He didn't much like anyone else in the compound, and strangely he had come to enjoy the idiosyncrasies of Hector Crispin. And watching the man made time move quickly.

Those around the table wore expensive clothes and maintained an air of elitism. Ryan looked at the nearest man to him. He guessed the suit probably cost the same as two months' rent. Where would they get their expensive suits now? Perhaps a tailor had been brought in on his flight. Perhaps a designer, too. Perhaps uniforms would become the norm. Ryan hoped they would be a flattering cut.

One of the members motioned to her aide and he poured her a glass of water from one of the decanters on the table. She didn't even say thanks. She was overweight. No uniform would cover her rolls. No outfit could ever be flattering.

"We are in a good position to begin stage two of the Athena Protocol, gentlemen. By now, you will all have identified pockets of organised resistance within your sectors. Civilian or military, we are to exercise all possible control over them. If they resist, then we destroy them. There can be no doubt, when the time is right, the world will know that we are in control. And of course, should we identify surviving members of the upper echelons of government or the military you will undertake all efforts to neutralise them."

"What about the maritime forces?" asked an elder member, his dark-rimmed glasses giving him the appearance of a stuffy librarian. "There is still a significant presence that we cannot move against."

Hector sipped from a glass of water. Ryan had poured it for him earlier, and Hector had thanked Ryan for the gesture.

Hector's hand shook. "Sooner or later they will run out of supplies and be forced to dock. When they do, we will be ready. Information is key. Observing and waiting for the right time to strike is paramount. You're right however to highlight the threat it might pose. For the moment I urge you all when acting against a target to use the creatures where possible. Withhold our manpower until necessary. We have identified a senior member of Cabinet in the Glasgow sector. We thought to approach him in order to bring him onside, however we now feel that he should be eliminated. This will be achieved very soon."

"And what of the situation in Glasgow? Your daughter?"

"She will endure. She knows what is at stake."

Ryan released his hold on the pen and cracked his knuckles, then shook the cramps out of his fingers. He was pleased to hear that Anastasia Hector, if that was her name, was capable of surviving out there. He looked forward to meeting her more and more every day. He gave his hands another shake. There would be a lot more writing. He hoped they had enough ink. The pandemic was merely the first stage.

***

Eric woke to the quiet and darkness of the early morning. Gemma lay next to him, her arm over his chest, an open sleeping bag draped across her hips and legs. She wore a thin vest, her chest rising and falling in a gentle rhythm. Sometime through the night, Skye returned to the tent and curled at their feet. Eric rubbed his face. What had he been thinking?

He moved her arm, placing it down by her side. She moaned lightly. Eric pulled on his trousers and boots. Skye looked up but finding little of interest, rolled back over to sleep.

"What time is it?" Gemma sat up.

"This was a mistake, Gemma. Things got confused."

She fell back to the bedding and threw a hand to her forehead. "You don't need to explain. We got a little drunk and fumbled around. It was nothing."

Eric pulled on his coat. "I want you gone from my tent. My family is out there for Christ's sake." He grabbed his rifle and headed out to the darkness.

***

Brutus and Silas left the tent.

"I'm going to need my guns back, boys," he said to the soldiers still guarding the way, and they were handed over.

"Much obliged." He felt more comfortable to be armed once again.

"That went well, don't you think?"

Brutus stuck a cigar in his mouth and lit it. He still wanted to stomp on Silas's head.

"It really doesn't matter what motivates you, Brutus. You agreeing to take survivors to the sanctuary is helping in one way, while ensuring your continued grasp to control The Owls' place. Everyone who is left will have something that motivates them."

"What's your point?"

"I suppose I don't have one. Just musing. Are we going back now?"

"I've no wish to be stuck out here any longer than I need to."

Several lanterns lit the way between the tents, some hanging from trees. They were dimmed low, giving off minimal light. The camp felt at rest. Most of the inhabitants hugged their fires, sitting close keeping out the night. Pitiful, thought Brutus. Weak and happy to let others protect them. A burden rather than an asset.

Brutus halted, staring at a figure moving through the trees.

"You know that girl?" asked Silas.

Brutus did not get a chance to answer. Gunfire opened up, close. The two dropped to their knees. Cries of alarm broke out in the camp.

***

Eric stormed to the camp latrine, cursing with every step. Gemma deserved better. She was just a kid, a scared kid. And Jacqui and the kids deserved better, too. What had he done?

He took a piss. Something moved beyond the latrine trench where light from the camp's lanterns could not reach. Whatever it was darted away. Eric had often spotted others taking a break from the routine of camp life at the edge of the camp, but his gut feeling was that this was a threat.

"Everything okay?" He pulled a lantern from a tree and tossed it over the shallow trench and into the dark. The spiralling light threw out flickers, enough to see.

An infected. Its jaw hung low at its chest. It launched from the shadows. Eric pulled his rifle up and opened fire, unleashing an automatic burst that ripped into the monster. It fell into the hole of shit and piss, but crawled forward on its elbows and grabbed for Eric's feet. Eric dodged the flailing hands and brought a heel down on its skull. The cranium gave way with a crunch.

Shouts erupted from back along the trail, followed soon after by gunfire. Heavy. Automatic. Sustained.

Eric ran back the way he came, clipping trees and stumbling over mounds of snow. Soldiers were loading weapons and hurrying toward the defensive perimeter. Armoured vehicles rumbled to life, great spurts of black smoke bursting from exhausts. Eric grabbed the magazine at his waist. It was empty. When he left Gemma in the tent he neglected to pick up his tactical vest or ammo pouches. He stuffed the empty magazine into his pocket.

Bright, burning flares shot high into the air, arching and descended into the outer snowfields. Eric reached the command tent. Outside, Alex Cunningham stood flanked by a brace of soldiers. Major Reid shouted orders to the vehicle crews, his sidearm drawn.

"We need to secure the perimeter," shouted Eric over the engines.

Reid grabbed Eric's arm. "We need every shooter out there. The sentry positions can't hold this number alone. We need to offer them fire support. We need to hold them at outer defences."

"They're coming from the west, too."

"Let me worry about that," the Major snapped. "Get some ammo and make yourself useful."

Alex was bundled into one of the armoured vehicles. Screams came from tents. One scream broke through all the others.

"Eric!"

***

It was not the first time Gemma had been spurned. She was not peeved, but perhaps minutely annoyed in the manner he departed. Surely he knew she acted selfishly for a moment of pleasure in this maddening place. She needed the closeness of someone, someone tall, strong, mature. And Eric always seemed to be the one rescuing her.

She made her way back toward her tent, and suddenly ducked in the fashion someone might when sensing a thunderclap overhead. Gunfire came from all around. She dropped to a knee and scuttled over to the base of a tree. Others scrambled from their tents. Some grabbed personal belongings or children. Others stood, rooted in fear and confusion.

Strong arms grabbed her and pulled her to her feet. She turned. She knew the face and that scar that ran down his face. But it had a fresher scar running the same length. Gemma tried to grab the knife in her boot. She'd give him a third cut to complain about.

Brutus seized her wrist, swallowing it up in one massive fist.

"Not this time, bitch." His breath was full of stale cigar. "You gave me something to remember you by in Aberdeen, remember?" He touched a finger to his face. It hadn't healed well. "Now it's time that I give you something in return, and I have something that'll fit your neck perfectly."

"No! Let me go!"

More gunfire. Closer this time.

Gemma screamed.

***

Brutus and Silas ran away from the sounds of attack with Gemma locked in Brutus's grip. They paused, Brutus patted down Gemma, searching her for hidden weapons. The lesson of Aberdeen was not lost on him. He touched a knife handle in her boot, pulled it out and threw it away into the snow.

"Give me a weapon," urged Silas.

"Shut up and move!"

Gemma screamed over and again. Brutus slapped her hard. She gave another scream and he hit her again, harder, and to the mouth.

The landing area was illuminated by two flares. Three infected were heading toward the landing zone.

"Give me a weapon," demanded Silas. "I'm not standing here with those things ready to eat everything around here."

The infected circled the helicopter.

Brutus pulled his combat knife free and threw it at Silas's feet, blade first. It speared the ground. He couldn't fire at the infected until they were away from the chopper. He pushed Gemma into Silas.

"She's full of tricks. Watch her."

Brutus sidestepped out from the cover of the trees. His boots crunched through the snow. The creatures veered away from the helicopter, making a direct line toward him. Brutus raised his AK-47 and waited, letting them get closer, letting them move away from his only means of escape.

Brutus fired, taking the first two down with expert aim. The third reached him, grabbed his weapon and pushed it down before ripping it free and tossing it aside. Brutus dashed back two steps, pulled his Glock, but the creature was on him. The thing was impossibly strong. They locked like a pair of wrestlers. Its jaws worked hard and fast aiming for his face. Brutus struggled hard to avoid those teeth. If he could just bring the gun to bear. But Brutus was in trouble. It was too strong.

The point of a knife sprang from the infected's throat. The creature dropped to the ground.

"You may thank me, Brutus, if you wish," said Silas.

"Where's the girl?"

Silas nodded to behind Brutus. Gemma lay in the snow, holding her ankle.

"I maimed her."

"Get the chopper ready to fly. I want us out of here before more of those things appear."

Behind them more flares descended down at the far side of the camp. Heavier guns fired, booming their payloads. Silas climbed into the helicopter. The rotors started to spin.

Brutus untied a length of rope that was strung up between trees. "I'm sorry I won't be able to do this properly, but I'm a little pressed for time. I've somewhere to be," he said to Gemma.

"Eric!" she screamed.

"Eric?" Brutus stood still. "What do you mean Eric?"

Gemma wept. "Please let me go."

"Eric Mann?"

"No," she whimpered.

Brutus stepped on her injured ankle and pushed.

"Yes! Yes!"

He withdrew his foot and laughed. "It's like a reunion of old friends." Brutus reached for her, the rope tight in his hands.

***

Eric ran toward the scream.

"Gemma?" The battle cancelled out his call.

In the trees not far away came an unnatural glow of red. Flares at the edge of the forest. Eric set off again. As he drew closer, the din of a helicopter's engine broke the sounds of weapon fire. He broke through the treeline and into the clearing. The scene made no sense. A helicopter hovered ten feet off the ground. Gemma sat slumped beneath it, a thick rope around her neck, the end attached to the aircraft. The downdraft caused snow to flurry about her. She grasped at the thick rope, pulling at the makeshift noose.

He called out to Gemma, but the roar of the engine stole the words. In the helicopter door sat Brutus, his legs dangling over the side. Brutus, Richard Desai, a one-time colleague of Eric's in Black Aquila. Now a murderer, betrayer and enemy to him.

Eric pulled his AR-15 up, aimed and pulled the trigger. Nothing. The magazine was empty. He threw the assault rifle down, and reached for his sidearm. Shots rang out from the helicopter and snow burst into the air at his feet. Brutus wagged his finger like a teacher scolding a pupil.

Gemma mouthed, "I'm sorry, Eric. I'm sorry."

Brutus pointed upward. The aircraft ascended pulling the rope tight and lifted Gemma from the ground. She kicked wildly, clawing at the rope at her neck. The helicopter went higher. Gemma twisted in the air. The helicopter hovered. Brutus's eyes were on Eric.

"No, Brutus! No! Let her go, you bastard!"

Gemma's arms dropped to her sides. The helicopter flew higher, and her legs stopped kicking.

The helicopter flew higher again, and the engine became a dull rumble. Gemma dropped from the great height, her body tumbling over, once then twice, the rope spiralling after her, and to Eric's ears, her fall to the ground made no sound.

***

Eric ran through the woods, running from one source of light to the next. An infected reared up from the tangle of a tent. Eric reversed the grip on his AR-15 and swung the weapon as a makeshift club. He struck the infected at the temple, and followed with another strike and then another. The infected went to ground. Eric stepped over it and delivered a final strike. It thrashed before falling silent. He dropped the rifle, not wanting to risk touching any of its blood. Eric stumbled away panting, and pressed on eager to reach the lines and the fighting. A group of six civilians moved toward him, going as a unit, all linking hands. One carried a lit gas lantern.

Eric raised a hand to them. "Where are you going?"

"We're getting out of here." It was the elderly man that had shown Eric around the campsite when he first arrived. The man clutched a thick branch as a weapon. "They're inside the camp."

"You can't leave the camp," said Eric, flatly. "It's not safe out there."

"And here is?"

"No, I don't mean that. They've been mining the approaches to the camp. You step outside the perimeter you stand a good chance of blowing yourself up."

"We're being murdered in here. We can't just wait to die." The man clutched the branch tighter. "Are you going to stop us?"

Eric shook his head and headed to the command tent. He rearmed himself with an SA80 and all the magazines he could carry. He loaded and checked the weapon, and ran to the edge of the camp. Eric leapt the short ditch and tumbled into the fortifications. He crawled to the lip and readied his weapon.

Wave upon wave of infected charged up the hill. Great bursts of dirt flew through the air as mines detonated. Arms and legs were ripped from torsos. None deterred the mob. More seemed to fill the gaps the mines created. Major Reid's men poured fire down the hill, tracers streaking through the night.

Warrior combat vehicles trundled free of the trees, bouncing out into the snowfields. Its 30mm cannon fired.

Eric had never seen so many infected. Perhaps thousands. How had they grown in such numbers away from the city?

Major Reid appeared, retreating uphill back to the defensive line. He dragged a wounded soldier, his legs and arms limp. Reid rolled next to Eric, the soldier tumbled after him.

"What happened to him?"

"He's bit. I thought he'd been hit by our fire."

"He's going to turn, you know that?"

The Major swore, placed his sidearm to the soldier's chest and fired a single shot into the heart.

A creature appeared above Eric. Reid shot it through the head before Eric could turn. It fell back. Eric dragged himself back to the edge of the earthwork. The press of infected was closer. Many now swarmed over the Warrior, beating at its armoured hull. Soldiers stabbed with bayonets and hit with rifle butts. But they could not match their strength.

Hands and teeth ripped their flesh and screams rang long. More infected appeared in the red light of the flares. Eric fired down on them, taking aim with each shot. Many fell only to rise, clamping hands over wounds. Reid grabbed the rifle that hang from dead soldier's shoulder and fired. He swore with each shot.

The line of infected stretched far in each direction.

"We need to fall back." Eric reloaded.

"To where?"

More mines exploded.

"Call in air support."

"Not gonna happen. They're committed elsewhere."

Eric considered fleeing back to the camp, grabbing Skye if he could find her, his pack and more ammo and leaving. But there was nowhere to run. The world around him was dying and the camp he fought to preserve represented the only hope to be maintained. The camp was his last tendril to the living world.

Two infected reached the defensive line. Eric pushed himself to his feet, reached out and yanked at the legs of the first. It stumbled and fell. Major Reid dropped his rife, pulled his sidearm out and blasted away at the creature before it had a chance to rise. The second infected leapt down, knocking the SA80 free of Eric's grasp. It lashed out, catching Eric on the chin. He stumbled back. The predator launched itself. Eric brought his arms up, covering his face. It crushed him in a bear hug, bringing its mouth close enough that Eric could hear the teeth snap. Its warm breath hit him. He struck out with his elbows doing little more than antagonising the creature. The creature's hands were at Eric's throat. He could not get air into his lungs.

How many people end like this?

It snapped at his arms, missing his skin by a hair's breadth.

The infected squeezed harder. Eric's eyes rolled back. Around him men died, torn apart by an unhuman foe. What was one more body among the many?

Those hands released Eric and the creature scrambled for the Major. Eric gasped for air and reached to the corpse next to him, pulled a bayonet free from the belt, and rolled to his feet. Eric wasted no time, got behind the infected and plunged the blade into the thing's spine. It speared all the way through. The infected dropped like a stone in a pond. It roared its frustration, clawing its way forward, dragging redundant legs behind. Major Reid kicked the thing in the head over and again until it stopped moving.

Another Warrior vehicle rumbled from the trees, turned sharply and fired down on the advancing horde. Bodies were blown into pieces. Eye sockets emptied. Skulls lost cheeks. Figures moved in the treeline. The civilians from the camp had armed themselves. They rushed to join the defence. A mortar team set up their weapon behind the main line of defence and began to fire.

Eric picked his SA80 up and blasted away, no aiming, no thought, just intent on dropping as many as he could. Others were doing the same. The added numbers were enough to thin the herd. No more creatures reached their lines. A platform of bodies stretched as far as Eric could see. Some still moved, most were still. The Warriors working in tandem fired at concentrations further ahead. The movement lessened. The gunfire lessened. The tide turned.

***

Silas piloted the helicopter. He had said little since they left the camp.

Killing the bitch who cut up his face provided Brutus with some fleeting satisfaction. If time was not against them he would have made her suffer like she deserved. Still, she was dead and he was alive.

"What will happen when we get back?" asked Silas.

"You just concentrate on getting us back in one piece."

"We shall be back soon, Brutus. We're just coming over Glasgow."

Spot fires in streets broke the city's darkness.

"Ah, Brutus, I think we have a problem."

"Why don't you just shut up for the rest of the journey?"

Silas pointed forward. Fire burned in the distance. "I believe that is our sanctuary."

"That's my goddamn building."

They flew closer then circled the building. It looked like the building had snapped in half, wreckage falling to the sides and destroying the protective wall. The fire was lessening, some areas simply smouldering ruins.

"What the hell happened to my building? Set us down."

"We do not know what's down there. It is not safe to land."

"Get us down there or I'll throw you out and do it myself."

"I cannot see enough to land this thing, Brutus."

"You can see fine. Land. Now!"

Silas did as was ordered and the helicopter touched down inside the walls. Brutus slid the door open, grasped the handrail and leaned out. The heat from the fire was intense.

"The Owls will pay for this, Silas. I'll make them pay for all of this."

"I don't think we can blame The Owls of Athena for this, Brutus. From what I understand I don't think they have the capability to employ firepower enough to bring down a building like this. You're a military man, too. I believe it may have been a missile strike, and only the military could launch an attack of this intensity. And whoever it was has killed the daughter of a senior Owl. Maybe they thought they were striking The Owls and not us. Wrong place, wrong time."

"What do we do now?" asked Silas.

"How many miles can you get out of the helicopter?"

Silas whistled a low sound as he considered. "One-hundred-and-fifty miles, if we're lucky."

"Prep for take-off."

"Good, I don't want to linger here much longer. The natives are getting restless."

Figures clambered over the fallen wall and wrecked vehicles.

The rotors of the helicopter started. Brutus gave one final look into the fire. He thought about offering words for his fallen comrades, but he knew the dead needed no consideration. Their problems were over.

***

Morning broke. Nobody moved from the defensive lines for fear that more infected would come. But none did.

Eric clutched his weapon to his chest. His body ached and his shoulder had seized up from bracing the rifle. Skye licked Eric's cheek, her tail busy with excitement. She was alive and had found her way to him in all the madness.

"Good girl," he said.

A solid kick came to Eric's foot.

Major Reid stood over him. "On your feet, soldier. You up for taking a walk?"

Eric gingerly rolled his shoulders encouraging both to relax. "Before I go anywhere I have a question."

"And?"

"Before the attack, there was a man who was in camp. A man you might know as Richard or Brutus."

"What about him?"

"He killed Gemma Findlay, one of the civilians here. He once worked for The Owls of Athena. I need you to promise me that when our paths cross again, you or your men won't stand in my way. He has to die."

"Are we not surrounded with enough death for you, Eric? Look around, the dead outnumber the living."

"It's personal."

"Let's talk about this another time."

Eric pushed himself up. Alex Cunningham stood just behind him.

The three men walked in silence over the defensive line and onto the snowfield. Alex covered his nose and mouth with a thick scarf, holding it tight. The snowfield was a bed of slaughter. Almost every square inch was layered with a corpse. The stench was unavoidable. Infected and non-infected rotted together in absolute equality, indistinguishable.

"I never dreamed anything in the world could be like this," said Alex. "We were brought to the brink this morning. On any other day, we would have been overcome."

"We lost too many good people," agreed Major Reid. "Men we can't afford to lose."

"This was no random attack. So many infected making their way out here far from any populated centre? They were baited because of this place." Eric pointed to Alex Cunningham. "What you've created here is a problem to The Owls of Athena. This camp and the people in it represent a splinter of the order they've torn apart and this is the result."

"You're right," said Alex. "Such a mass movement into this area was not thought possible. But, as for me and what I do here, I'm just trying to do the right thing. This was never my intention."

"Then make it official," said Eric. "Announce yourself. If you are all that's remaining of the government then you need to exercise some authority. Bring the remaining military elements under one direction. If you want to help the people, you need to think larger than this camp."

"He's right," said Major Reid. "We no longer have the manpower to maintain a presence here. We need to coordinate with whoever is left. This is war."

"It's a war against the Carrion Virus and The Owls of Athena," said Eric.

"Yes," said Alex Cunningham. "This, what's happened here I never thought possible. So much death. So much destruction. Everything we've lost. This is war. It's one I'm not sure we can win. I fear something terrible. This war will last forever."

THE END

CHECK OUT OTHER GREAT
APOCALYPSE BOOKS

XY
by D.S. Lillico

An iron fortress protected by automated gun turrets is the only world Elsie has ever known.

When tragedy strikes, Elsie is forced to leave the sanctuary of her home and out into a brutal new world. A post-apocalyptic wasteland filled with savage mutants.

Hunted and alone Elsie stumbles into the care of a giant named Punch, but the world is now full of worse things than giants. Cannibals are starving, bandits are roaming and war is coming.

Elsie's arrival plunges the new-world further into darkness... and is there really something hidden inside of her?

SANCTUARY
by Ian Page

Deeta Nakshband, a Connecticut physician is attacked by a local surgeon while on duty in the hospital. Her friend, Janelle Jefferson, has similar experiences in Miami. Both of them become aware of an increasingly violent world as acts of isolated brutality escalate into civil unrest. They grapple with their paranoia as family members and coworkers become dangerously unpredictable. Worldwide, military units go rogue, war begins in Korea and cities implode as people slaughter each other in the streets. Martial law is declared in an attempt to maintain order. People are arrested, detainment camps are set up and interrogations end with tragic consequences as modern civilization crumbles. Deeta and Janelle band together with family friends and coworkers to save each other and find sanctuary.

 SEVEREDPRESS

 facebook.com/severedpress
 twitter.com/severedpress

CHECK OUT OTHER GREAT APOCALYPSE BOOKS

WHITE OUT
by Eric Dimbleby

An apocalyptic snowstorm sweeps the globe. Experts predict this freak storm will be "The New Ice Age." Electricity is gone, as are all forms of communication and road travel. As each member of a divided family tries to survive in their own way, they must deal with a snow-driven madness that has gripped the underlying evil in the hearts of men. In an epic struggle to get home and reunite, they will find that terror lies around every snow drift... and even in their very own backyard.

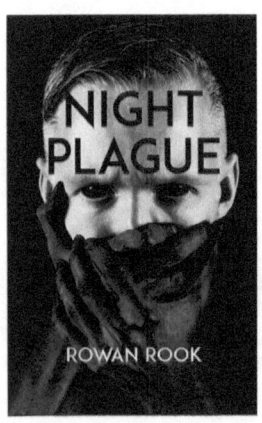

NIGHT PLAGUE
by Rowan Rook

Humankind will soon be extinct. A mysterious pandemic cut through two-thirds of the population in just four short years, and within another four, it will decimate everything – and everyone – left.

The last days are ticking by, relentless and ruthless, and the reclusive Mason Mild finds himself torn between a peaceful end and a brutal immortality. Between his hopeless, but comfortable days with his family, and something new...something violent and wild.

Have the fang marks above his heel dealt him an early demise or a second birth?

CHECK OUT OTHER GREAT APOCALYPSE BOOKS

THE DEAD FAMILIAR
by J.D. McKenna

In the twilight hours of a failing world, one man seeks to bring his loved ones to safety. Jack Hightower: Marine, bar-keep, and doomsday prepper. He knows of the coming calamity, and on the final night of an old world he seeks a new beginning.
This is the story of that night, the tale of how Jack and his survivor's colony in the north came to be.

DOMINION
by Doug Goodman

Dominion has been taken from man. Now, six friends must cross an apocalyptic wasteland dominated by a hell's menagerie of mega-fauna. Their middle-class suburban skills are no longer applicable to the world they live in. To find a safe haven in this world they will need to develop a new set of survival skills and fight the mutated denizens of the animal kingdom for every step of their terrifying journey.